I AM IN HERE

CRESTON MAPES

STAND ALONE THRILLERS

I Am In Here

Nobody

SIGNS OF LIFE SERIES

Signs of Life

Let My Daughter Go

I Pick You

Charm Artist

Son & Shield

Secrets in Shadows

THE CRITTENDON FILES

Fear Has a Name

Poison Town

Sky Zone

ROCK STAR CHRONICLES

Dark Star: Confessions of a Rock Idol

Full Tilt

PRAISE FOR *I AM IN HERE*

"I haven't been truly gobsmacked by a book in a long time, and *I Am in Here* literally took my breath away! The premise of this suspense thriller, set in a volatile family predicament that seems to go from bad to worse by the minute, is brilliantly told in part by the brain-injured son no one knows is still "in there." Hale's perspective keeps us quite literally holding our breath and anxiously turning pages all the way to the end. Creston is the most gifted suspense writer I know; how he ratchets up the drama blows me away. I loved this book!" — **Amazon Reviewer**

"*I Am In Here* will hook you in the first chapter and keep you reading until the last. The book gave me more insight into those with traumatic brain injuries but also how their families are affected. Loved this book!" — **Amazon Reviewer**

"I absolutely loved this book and could not put it down. The tension and excitement held me until the end. I will be thinking about this story, the characters, and the resolutions for many days to come. Mr. Mapes, never quit writing!" — **Amazon Reviewer**

"*I Am In Here* is a thought-provoking book. Until we have walked this road, we have no idea what these families face. The expenses alone can push us to consider options we would never explore otherwise. I loved the way the author presented these dilemmas and the desperate measures pursued. I highly recommend this book." — **Amazon Reviewer**

"*I Am In Here* had me hooked from the first chapter and I couldn't turn the pages fast enough! Hale's struggle gave me pause and made me see traumatic brain injury patients in a different light and the desperation shown within the family dynamic is heart-breaking. Once again, Creston succeeds in bringing a compelling story to life." — **Amazon Reviewer**

This is a work of fiction. Names, characters, organizations, places, events, and incidents are either products of the author's imagination or are used fictitiously. Any resemblance to actual persons, living or dead, or actual events is purely coincidental.

No part of this book may be reproduced or stored in a retrieval system, or transmitted in any form or by any means, electronic, mechanical, photocopying, recording, or otherwise, without express written permission of the publisher.

Scripture quotations from: *New American Standard Bible* (NASB) 1960, 1977, 1995 by the Lockman Foundation. *The Holy Bible,* New International Version (NIV) 1973, 1984 by International Bible Society.

Copyright © 2022 Creston Mapes, Inc
Published by Rooftop Press

Thanks to Chuck 'The Closer' Pardoe and to Lujack Ewell for their timely creativity.

Cop buddy Mark Mynheir, as always, thanks for the inside scoop on police procedures.

Special thanks to my incomparable early reader team for your time and insights: Patty Mapes (wink, wink), Vicki Burke, Gail Mundy, Diane Moody, Lynnelle Murrell, Rachel Savage, and Ginger Aster.

1

HALE

I can see, you know.

And I can hear. *Oh, can I hear.* It's become my secret weapon—my hearing. Even from across the room, people's hushed voices register with pitch-perfect clarity in what they think is my dead brain. *People's ears are better than you think; remember that the next time you're about to blab some mindless comment to your pal.*

I'm quite certain my hearing has gotten keener since the . . . you know what. It's probably my ears compensating for the other abilities that have been stripped from me. Honestly, it's like I'm wearing one of those secret ear amplifiers they're always pushing on one of the shopping channels.

Don't get me started on home shopping channels. I could be the poster boy for 'As Seen on TV.' The giant widescreen at the foot of my fancy 'hospital' bed is on 24/7 and, for some reason, everyone around here—except my best friend, Gilbert—thinks I love the home shopping shows. Probably because I stare at them with glazed eyes and mouth gaping like the Grand Canyon. What they don't realize is that I'm not enamored with the shows, instead I'm thinking, *can anyone possibly believe these cheap gadgets really work?*

Don't get me wrong, I love Shark Tank. And I *love* Laurie, the glamorous blond on the panel. She does put her products on home shopping channels. It's just that, when you watch that stuff as much as I do, you start to realize—

Wait a minute.

Voices.

In the kitchen.

Dad and someone else.

Not Sandra.

A visitor... a man.

As the sound of the visitor's low, gravelly voice registers, my lanky body involuntarily jolts, and arches. My head cranes toward the unwanted stranger.

Sebastian.

My bony knees jerk up toward my chest. If possible, this stiff body would shrink up and coil into the fetal position. My hands, already bent to the insides of the wrists, jam up beneath my chin and into my chest.

I hear myself begin to cry.

Can't help it.

My pulse pounds in my neck and temples.

I am groaning loudly, involuntarily.

What is he doing here this late? It must be after ten and it's a blizzard outside.

My dad and Sebastian enter my room from the kitchen speaking in low tones. Dad takes the husky man's huge winter coat and hangs it on a hook on the coat rack, but it starts to tip from the weight. Dad catches it and decides to rest the coat on the seat of a nearby chair.

The hairy wolf Sebastian rolls up his sleeves while fixing his animal eyes on me, ignores my violent flinch, and heads right for me.

Brace for it...

Sebastian jostles me like a dog and rubs the top of my head with the tips of his hard fingers like he's scrubbing stains out of a rug.

Ouch!

I hear myself moan, which he mistakes for a laugh, which he's done each time he's been here.

"See that?" He cackles and looks back at Dad, who's standing sheepishly with his fingers locked in front of him as he stands by the door to my bedroom, which is really our back porch, which Dad enclosed and made into my spacious quarters after the . . . you know what.

"He missed me!"

Not quite, Sebastian.

He squeezes the back of my neck with ice-cold hands and a vice-like grip, then does the same to my shoulders, forcing my groan to sound desperate and my face to flush.

I want to rebuke him, slap his fat face, but you realize by now, I am unable to do that.

He smells like sausage and fails to look me in the eyes or speak to me, but addresses my dad, instead.

"Does he have this reaction with anyone else?" Sebastian says. "I mean, look at him; he's thrilled. I made his day." He is an overweight, but rock solid, uncouth man with wrists the size of logs, curly gray-black hair, furry black eyebrows, and a jet-black mustache, which I'm certain he dyes; it's hideously obvious. *Why would his wife let him out like that?*

"How old is he again?" Sebastian asks.

"His name is Hale," Dad says. "Eighteen."

"And he's been like this how long?"

My dad looks so uncomfortable, not only with the questions, but with Sebastian's very presence. Dad is nervous, I can tell.

"About a year," Dad says.

"Car wreck?"

"That's right."

It wasn't exactly a car wreck . . .

"You have to feed him by hand every meal?"

"He's fed with a g-tube. He can't eat by mouth."

Duh, Sebastian!

Sebastian mutters and cusses. "That's just not right. Don't you ever wish, you know . . . he would've just . . ."

Does this jerk not know I'm within two feet of him?

My dad glances at me, swallows hard, and says, "No. No. Never. My gosh, he's my son."

"You have another kid, right?"

Dad shifts and nods, about to blow a gasket.

"Daughter?"

"Uh huh."

"How old again?"

"Twenty."

"Mmm. She still lives here?"

Dad's mouth seals shut, his eyes close, and he nods as if offering himself up as a sacrificial lamb, volunteering to take this punishment, for what reason I don't know.

"And Sandra works, right? Doesn't she work out of the house?"

"I think you know all this, Sebastian. Right? Don't you?" Dad is annoyed now.

After a moment of disbelief that Dad has talked back to him, Sebastian's large head and shoulders inch back, and he chuckles. "Alright, alright, enough small talk. Let's get down to business then." Sebastian squeezes my crippled, chapped hands too hard and saunters back over to where my dad is standing.

"How are we looking, Douglas?" Sebastian lowers his voice. "You got something for me, or what?" Sebastian wears shiny, loose gray dress slacks pulled up high at his thick waist, a black long-sleeved dress shirt, shiny black belt and shoes, and a gold bracelet and matching necklace the size of bike chains. He also wears a thick gold wedding band.

What the heck is a gangster like this even doing in our house?

"You want some coffee?" Dad rubs his hands together. "I can do some instant."

Sebastian waves him off. "Money, Douglas. That's what I'm here for. Money. You're overdue. We've been patient; more than patient."

Dad shifts slightly, putting Sebastian's wide frame between us so I can't see Dad's face. I think Dad knows I can hear—and understand; he's one of the few. Luckily the volume on the TV is low. I hear Dad explain in a humble tone that he needs more time.

"That's it." Sebastian comes to a sudden boil, his fat fingers curled stiff like claws at his sides. "This is going to the next level, Frodele, and there isn't anything I can do about it. You understand? I like you. I feel for your boy—your situation. But this is it, *tonight.*"

"Take my car, please," Dad says. "And I've got tools, lots of expensive tools. I've told you . . . and jewelry, my wife's—"

"We are not a pawn shop! Cash only. Tonight. You knew the terms when you got into this gig."

Notice, Dad hasn't offered the conversion van with the handicap lift for when they have to wheel me to the specialists. That's the kind of guy he is, committed to me to the bitter end.

"I just need a few more days, please, I promise—"

"You said that ten days ago and ten before that. You promised you'd have it and I'm here for it." Sebastian has a stiff finger in Dad's face. "I swear, next time it is not going to be me, and it is not going to be a social call. I feel for you, Douglas. You think you're protecting your kid and your family, but you're not. You're going to bring grief on this home. You're leaving my people no choice."

"They're not going to get their money by hurting me, Sebastian. Don't they understand that?"

Sebastian turns and stares right at me, the reflection of the glowing TV screen shining in his black eyes. "Who said anything about hurting you?"

2

HALE

It's late the same night. Jimmy Kimmel is interviewing Lady Gaga. I can't stand him. I adore her—ever since that movie with her and Bradley Cooper, *A Star is Born*. Saw that in the theater before the . . . you know what.

But I'm so sick of the TV. I wish my peeps would simply turn the thing off occasionally. I don't know where they get the idea I need it on to pacify me around the clock. It's like trying to sleep at the foot of a giant LED billboard for a used car dealership, blazing like neon in the dead of night.

Sebastian almost got his red Cadillac stuck in the snow when he left a little while ago. I had to laugh. But he rocked that sucker back and forth until it came roaring out in a cloud of exhaust, sliding sideways, then chugging into the frigid night.

I can see everything from this window. As I said, this used to be a screened porch. It's off the back of our old house and it sits up high because the back of the property drops off into the woods. There's a creek down there that we used to play in. Dad and my real mom would cook us bacon and eggs over a small fire out there while the three of us kids played in the stream.

God, how times have changed.

Our property is situated on a narrow country road with a leaning green metal mailbox and several acres of land, just like all the others out here. But we can be in downtown Akron in five minutes, and to Cleveland in twenty. If you've never been to northeast Ohio, we're talking about snow and slush and salt and rust and ugly gray skies six or seven months out of the year. Ah, but the rest of the year is pure heaven—bold blue skies, shimmering lakes, pleasant summer evenings with the smell of fresh cut grass in the air, and the sweetest corn-on-the-cob you've ever tasted.

Dad somehow convinced Sebastian to give him two more days. After Sebastian left, Dad disappeared into the low-lit house for several minutes before he came back and fed me my 'midnight snack'—via g-tube and food pump. Everything is g-tube and food pump.

What I wouldn't give for a fourteen-ounce ribeye.

Anyway, Dad was unusually quiet; just sat next to me, stared down into my eyes, and stroked my curly hair while the warm, white liquid food coiled its way along the clear tube into the port near my bellybutton.

Dad usually talks with me, like a real person, as if I'm really still in here. He's one of the few. Tonight, however, he just stared at me, his own brown eyes glistening. A deep valley of concern, perhaps even desperation, carved lines in his forehead and in the crevice between his eyes. It isn't like him to worry and to say nothing. Usually, he at least tries to be strong and positive, no matter what the challenge.

Don't give up, Dad. Please, hang in there. You can't stop believing for a miracle. That's what I tried to tell him with my eyes. *I need you, Dad.*

He's gone now, either to bed or to work on something in his shop in the basement; it's therapy for him to plan a project, measure, saw, and build.

I close my eyes, wanting sleep to come, but still seeing the glow of the giant screen. I know it's hard to believe an upstanding guy like my dad would get into major debt with a lowlife like Sebastian and "his people," but you've got to understand, I'm expensive.

After the . . . you know what, I was in intensive care at Akron General for months. Then the Neurological Institute at Cleveland Clinic. Then numerous attempts at rehab with various brain injury specialists. And, of course, there were all the expenses from Nathaniel's funeral; I can't even go there right now.

When I came home, they had to install a sidewalk and ramp leading to the back porch—now my bedroom (a complete remodel). They had to get a special hospital bed, tilt table, and all kinds of other equipment, not to mention a plethora of medicine, special food, a part-time nurse, the list goes on.

I know Dad got a loan from the bank at one point, but how much would they loan him? We could be in debt hundreds of thousands of dollars for all I know. Isn't there something the government can do about it? Especially, having lost Nathaniel, and ending up with me in this condition?

Have a little sympathy, people!

Did you ever dare to ask yourself what might happen to your faith if something like this were to happen to you? I'll come right out and be straight up with you, my faith has faltered. Ever since the day of the... well, I'll come out and say it—bus crash.

Our church youth group was returning from a retreat at Salt Fork State Park. It was one of those rare, mountaintop experiences. I'd never felt happier or closer to God. You've heard that overused cliché, "rededicated" yourself to God? Well, I'd actually done that. Nothing public. Just between me and him. We were closer than we'd ever been. I was ready to go live out my faith.

On the trip home late at night, a thirty-seven-year-old named Gordon Blackstone hit a patch of black ice, crossed the center line in his Chevy pickup truck, and swiped our bus. We lost control and went off a bridge forty feet into a ravine. My little brother, Nate, died on impact. I ended up with what doctors are calling a severe traumatic brain injury, better known around here as TBI. My best friend Gilbert suffered a serious leg injury and now walks with a slight limp. Gordon Blackstone didn't have a scratch and no charges were filed, because he'd been driving the speed limit.

Unfortunately, people look at my rigid, crippled body and they have no clue that I'm in here.

They think I'm a vegetable.

Such an *ugly* term, isn't it?

Vegetable.

I AM IN HERE

Really? You would call another human being that?

I am a young man, people. I am not a tomato or a squash or a rusting head of lettuce. Eighteen years old, to be exact, the last time someone cared enough to show me a calendar.

But I'm in here, okay? *I'm in here!*

God knows. He and my best friend Gilbert know. Now, my older sister, Veronica, and my favorite nurse, Jasmine, and my dad—they *act* like they know I'm still in here. But the verdict's still out on whether they genuinely believe it or whether they're just pretending. But Gilbert knows.

The problem, as you've gathered by now, is that I have no way of expressing anything to anyone. Oh, they've had all kinds of experts in here, trying to make me blink and nod and squeeze and wiggle—and jab the red and green lighted buttons. But I can't do any of it. It's one big disconnect between what I *want* to do, and what I actually *can* do.

For instance, when I finally muster the will to speak, it either comes out like a long, low, creepy gasping for air, or the wheezing cry of an invalid with chronic emphysema. Sometimes the odd noises I make are nothing more than loud, grotesque, screeching groans that build and roll and build and roll until there's not one iota of air left in my lungs. A howling idiot is what I must sound like.

I hate to say this, because it makes me terribly sad, but people pity me. They pity my family for having to care for me. It's all truly depressing.

Want to know what *really* hurts? When my stepmom Sandra—aka, Cruella De Vil—actually mutters to visitors that my condition is "pitiful." She uses that word. Now, I don't have a thesaurus handy but to me that word means 'pathetic,' 'sorry,' and possibly even 'wretched.'

I try not to be judgmental. I try to put myself in her shoes and imagine what it would be like to have to care for me. You see, Cruella (Sandra), came into our lives *before* the bus crash. I was about sixteen when she met my dad. So, she didn't bargain for any of this caregiver drama. Ever since the awful day of the accident, everything has been different. Think of it—my dad lost a son that day (Nate) and the other (yours truly) became an invalid. Dad's relationship with Sandra tanked.

My real mom died when I was fifteen. I can't even describe what a beautiful human she was. Like that country song says, she was "one of the good ones." She was the one for my dad. That's when he was legit happy.

Now he's struggling just to keep his head above water.

I do my best to forgive the mean ones and relish the time with the ones who understand me, especially Gilbert. He'll be here tomorrow. His visits are my lifeline. They're golden. You'll see.

Okay, enough of that rabbit trail. My original point was that it's not like Dad doesn't have a steady job. He's a mail carrier for the U.S. Postal Service. His route is in Fairlawn—nice homes, good people. And, although she didn't want to, Sandra's taken a part-time job as a medical transcriber, playing doctors' audio recordings, and transcribing them into documents on the computer. She does it right from the next room at a wall desk my dad built for her in the kitchen.

Wait a second . . . from the adjoining kitchen I hear arguing.

It's Dad and Sandra.

"You've had *enough*," Dad barks in a stressful tone. "That's not going to help anything."

Sandra's a drinker, you see. Or, should I say, she's *become* one since the accident.

"What *is* going to help, Douglas? Huh? We're going to lose this place."

"Give me that," he says with a grunt.

She screams.

Glass shatters.

Sandra shrieks with canned laughter. "I'll just get another while you clean that up."

"Your getting smashed isn't helping anything!" Dad yells.

"It's helping me! It's helping me get numb from this *nightmare* I walked into."

I can hear the broom.

My dad is sweeping up the bottle or glass that broke.

I hear ice from the freezer clink into a glass.

"You should have one of these, Douglas," Sandra says with a slur.

"It'd help—take away the pain. Dull the senses a bit. Come on, let me pour you one."

Dad says something softly that I cannot understand.

"Suit yourself."

A bottle slams onto the counter.

Seconds later, a shadow falls over me.

Sandra enters my room and says, "Well, well, well—look who's still wide awake."

3

HALE

Sandra walks over clutching the glass of booze in both hands, stops next to my bed, and looks at me with her big brown eyes.

My body jerks. The knees go up. My curled hands press inward against my chest and up against my chin. All involuntary.

She swirls the ice and liquor, then takes a drink. Her head tilts sideways as she chews ice and stares at me.

I hear myself wheeze.

I can understand what my dad saw in her. She's got a pretty face. Her skin is fair and freckles dot her pink cheeks. Her hair is thick and reddish brown. She has put on weight in the past year, especially in her hips. Tonight, she looks like she's going to a Jason Aldean concert. She's wearing a navy winter vest over a white sweater that has one of those huge collars. She's got on new, stiff-looking dark blue jeans and gray cowboy boots.

She is so totally unlike my real mom.

She sets her drink down on a coaster by the window, picks up the soft, white diaper cloth that always rests over the bedrail, and wipes the drool from the corner of my mouth. She tugs and straightens my sheets and blanket. She looks up to see if Dad is within earshot.

"You see what you've gotten us into now?" Sandra says softly as she moves from my bed to a laundry basket that sits on a table nearby. Jasmine did a load today but never got around to folding it.

Sandra begins to do so. "We're going to lose this property because of you." She snaps each shirt and towel and folds them neatly. "I've tried my best to make this work, Hale, but your dad's changed. My gosh, he's a different man than the one I married." She speaks in almost a whisper so only I can hear. It's almost as if she's thinking aloud because I know she doesn't believe I'm in here. "He's literally a different person. Who wouldn't be? First, he loses a wife. Then a son. And he's left with Mr. Vegetable."

I cringe and jolt like someone who's been electrocuted.

She sighs.

"You should be in a home someplace."

She stops folding and stares at me. She goes over and takes a big swig of her beverage and sets it down. She sniffs and stands there, crunching ice and evaluating me.

She approaches, leans close, and whispers with a boozy breath, "We keep you alive, you know. If we didn't feed you, you'd starve to death. Do you understand that?"

My face burns and my eyes fix on hers like lasers.

"I swear, sometimes I think you can understand me."

She rests her hands on mine. Hers are warm and soft. Mine are cold, stiff, chapped, and deformed.

"I'm not giving up on my marriage yet." She looks toward the doorway, makes sure we are alone, and bends closer. "I'm willing to do *anything* to improve the situation with your dad."

She smiles and ruffles my hair.

I squawk.

Sandra examines her fingernails, then begins to chew viciously at the cuticle on one of her thumbs like a dog gnawing at a meaty bone.

Dad walks quietly into the room and comes over to my bed.

"Hey champ," he says.

Sandra returns to her beverage and takes a swig.

"I forgot to tell you, that preacher called again," Sandra says, crunching.

Huh?

What's this?

Dad hasn't set foot in a church since Mom died three years ago.

"Did you ever call him back?" Sandra says.

"I forgot," Dad says.

"What's he want? Certainly not money." Sandra chuckles at her own joke.

"I'll take care of it."

"I gave him your cell so he'd quit calling the house when I'm working."

"Fine."

Oh man, would I love it if Dad started going to church again.

But the chances of that are about as good as the Browns winning the Super Bowl.

We grew up in church. It was the focal point of our lives. Such happy memories. Back then, Mom and Dad were devoted to their faith. In fact, they met at a Christian retreat in Dayton when they were teenagers. They married after college and at age 24 mom gave birth to Veronica. I came along two years later (middle child syndrome), and Nathaniel was the caboose. The three of us kids loved Sunday School, then the youth programs. Church was our lives.

There was so much light and laughter in our house. Mom and Dad insisted we kids get along, love each other, and look out for one other. Each night, one of them would read us Bible stories on the carpeted steps, then pray with us.

I often think how utterly sick Mom would be if she knew Dad had turned his back on God soon after she died.

It makes *me* sick.

I'm sure she knows. I believe she's in heaven looking down on us. I really do.

Mom was beautiful—inside and out. Her name was Cindy and she was radiant. Her shiny blond hair always smelled like flowers. Her smile was like the sun. She was kind and gentle, yet firm. Very upbeat and confident. Extremely generous; always thinking of others. She had faith that could move mountains. She wasn't afraid of anything. She brought us up to be self-sufficient. And she was kind to a fault; my dad still says that.

I don't know how else I can say it—Mom was *torn* from us.

It started with back pain, which she laughed off as 'getting old.' As was her personality, she'd helped move a family into a shelter and thought she'd wrenched her back lifting heavy boxes. But then one morning she woke up terribly jaundiced. Dad rushed her to the doctor. By the time she got thoroughly checked out, it was too late. The pancreatic cancer had reached stage four—advanced. It had already silently spread to her liver and bones, and she was given only weeks to live.

Talk about a rock—she never lost faith.

She never stopped smiling—and laughing. She had the most winsome laugh.

We prayed for a miracle. All of us did. Our whole church did. Heck, people prayed who we didn't even know, thanks to Veronica's efforts on social media.

But the miracle never came.

Not even close.

Mom was buried in Shaker Heights near her childhood home where her parents still lived. They both survived her. She was only forty-four. The funeral is vivid to me. Dad was numb. It was as if his body was present, but his spirit had left him. He was like a ghost. He said nothing. He did nothing—for weeks.

Veronica, Nate, and I looked to him for hope, guidance, strength, and purpose.

He gave us none.

Instead, he'd curled up in his own little world of grief and bitterness.

He was eventually let go from the shipping company where he'd worked for sixteen years.

Our neighbors down the street, the Spencers, came through in Dad's place. They made sure we got to services on Sunday and to all our youth activities. They had kids close to our ages: Gilbert, my best friend to this day, and his sister, Ellie, upon whom I've always had the world's biggest crush.

"So what, you giving religion a try again?" Sandra's words to Dad snap me out of my daydream. "Pull some strings with the Big Cheese?"

I shift uncomfortably.

Dad ignores her and goes about washing my feeding equipment at the sink.

"That's got to be one of the biggest shams in history." She plunks down in a chair by the window with a grunt and slurps at her drink. "There you were, at that church every time the doors were open, serving, giving all your money, and what happens? How were you rewarded?"

"Enough Sandra," Dad says without looking at her.

"If you go back, you're the most gullible, *weak* person alive."

There was so much venom oozing from her that I again racked my brain trying to figure out how Dad had ended up with her. *Was she his curse for turning his back on God?*

Dad turns the water off, dries his hands, and turns to face Sandra. "Don't worry. I'm not going back." He leans back against the counter and folds his arms.

"What are you going to do about Sebastian, the money?"

Dad stares at her, then looks at me, but says nothing.

"You've got two days."

"I'm well aware of that."

"These are not good people, Douglas."

"I know that, too."

"What do you think they're going to do—if you don't have the money?"

Dad looks at me. "Let's not talk about this in front of Hale. Are you ready for bed?"

"Oh, come on, Douglas. Face reality! He can't understand us. I know you know he can't."

I jolt. Then I hear myself roar with a dreadful sound of agony.

"Why do you think he does that?" Dad says. "He understands what you're saying, Sandra. You're the one who can't face reality."

Sandra laughs and drains the last of her drink.

She slumps over and stares at Dad, shaking her head. "How long are we going to keep doing this, Douglas?" She pauses. "Haven't you had enough of this?" When she says this, she tosses her hands up at me and all of my special equipment.

Dad stares off, perhaps weighing her words.

"We were happy," she says. "I helped you get over Cindy, didn't I? We were in love. We had a good thing."

Dad turns to her. "We did. Then life happened. And here are."

"Yeah, and you're not the same person I married. You have to admit that. You're bitter to the core."

"Oh, and *you're* the same person *I* married?" Dad recoils. "You're a raging alcoholic. You've let yourself go—"

"How dare you! You're a pathetic excuse for a man. You're always preoccupied. There's never any spontaneity. You're no fun anymore. You won't snap out of it. I've given it plenty of time, Doug."

"Oh, so you're ready to bail. Is that it?"

She stands and glares at him. "I'm ready for *something* to change. I think we can still make it. But we need to make some *drastic* changes. When you're ready for that, you let me know."

Ho-ly-cow.

She's talking about me.

4

HALE

It's early in the morning. The light outside is mostly from the brightness of the snow on the ground. The trees look dark and wet.

I smell coffee and eggs. Dad's been up awhile.

I can feel the cold from the window. Everything outside is still—frigid, clear, and frozen like a picture. It's got to be below ten degrees. The foot of snow on the ground has formed a hard, icy crust on top, the kind I used to enjoy punching my boots through. It's not good packing snow, because, underneath the icy top the snow is like powder; it doesn't pack at all.

Frozen drifts are rolled four feet high against Dad's tool shed. The bird feeder suction-cupped to my window has formed icicles five inches long.

I hear a car.

Probably . . . yep, Jasmine, my nurse, chugging up the driveway in her old Ford Bronco, steam billowing from the tailpipe. The Bronco is blue, but you can barely tell, because it's covered in snow, salt, and dirt, with huge chunks of ice hanging behind the rear wheel wells. It's that way because she has to park outside. She lives in an apartment down in the valley.

My back itches so badly. Of course, I can't scratch it.

I sigh and try to think of something else, but I hear myself give off a low, rattling sound.

In my condition you're forced to get used to denying yourself. You want a heck of a lot of things, but you get virtually none of them. After a while, you just learn to . . . exist. It sometimes makes me think of how Jesus must have felt when he knew he was headed to the cross. *Like a sheep going to the slaughter. Silent. He did not open his mouth.*

If Jesus could do that, I can endure this.

I'm not done.

Just like he was resurrected, I'm waiting to be raised up.

I don't want to stay like this. *I can't.* It will drive me insane.

I believe he can heal me. If he wants to.

Please heal me. Help Dad get out of the mess he's in. Bless my time with Gilbert today. I'm counting on you.

Jasmine has made her way in. I hear her talking with Dad in the kitchen. He's probably taking her coat and pouring her coffee. It dawns on me this is not her usual day. It's Tuesday. Gilbert's coming. I love Jasmine, but Gilbert and I need to be alone. Jasmine was just here yesterday. She usually comes Monday, Wednesday, and Friday. I'm starting to feel grouchy.

"Go-od morn-ing sun-shine." She always says it in the same way, like a little song. "I bet you're surprised to see me."

Dad follows her into my room, carrying her favorite mug of Sandra's—the dark blue Game of Thrones. "You're getting a haircut today, bud," he says.

I instantly jerk and then give my biggest caw.

I *hate* haircuts with a capital *H*.

"Jasmine can't come tomorrow, so we had her come two days in a row."

I continue to moan and squirm.

"It's okay," Dad says. "She's not going to be in your way when Gilbert comes."

She can't be in the room, that's what Dad doesn't understand.

We need privacy!

Jasmine is a whirlwind. Wearing her light green scrubs and black-and-orange Nikes, she quickly flushes my g-tube with water and gets the food pump started, apologizing for her cold hands, and prepares my toothbrush.

Right after my accident, even though Dad wasn't going to church, friends from there prepared pouches of pureed food for me—lentils, black beans, potatoes, bananas. We always had a freezer full of single meals that Dad or Veronica or Sandra could thaw and feed me through the g-tube. After a while—probably because none of us were going to church there anymore—the gourmet meals came to a screeching halt. Now I get the packaged stuff.

Jasmine smells like lotion. She has a buzz cut afro that's sassy short. Her skin is light brown, and she has plump, pink cheeks. The bit of makeup she wears makes her face glow and her fingernails are always some neat, shiny color. She's only about five feet tall, so she sometimes steps up on a footstool to reach me.

"Open up," she says, holding the toothbrush in front of my face.

I hear myself shriek.

"Boy, you are in a sour mood today. Are you not glad to see me?"

I protest in frustration because I don't want her to think I'm not glad to see her, but it comes out like the miserable sound of someone struggling to breathe while being strangled.

"Ah, that's better." She brushes my teeth hard and thoroughly. "Lean over. Try to spit for me." She holds a small plastic cup, but I can only lean over and drool into it.

"Good man." She wipes my mouth and is off to the sink.

"Want to know a secret?" She stops to sip her coffee, then whispers across the room, "I've been dating someone."

I flinch and give the strangled laugh, because she's always talking about meeting her knight in shining armor, but nothing ever happens.

Somehow she knows my laugh. "I know, right?" she says. "We met online. His name's Reggie. Never been married. Realtor. Seems very successful. Last night was our fourth date. We met at Jade Garden, the Chinese place on West Market. Now, you don't go telling your dad or Veronica."

Jasmine dries her hands with a towel, leans against the counter, and stares at me. "You're really listening, aren't you?"

That made me flinch.

"He's probably a foot taller than me. In good shape. Loves to hike and walk at different parks. Plays in some volleyball league, and

I AM IN HERE

softball." Jasmine opens several low cupboards until she finds what she's looking for. Then she kneels down and pulls out the box of haircut equipment while she continues to fill me in. "He asked me about my past. I was honest with him. Told him about my marriage to TJ—how he turned out to be a porn addict. You know, I figure honesty is the best policy."

TJ was an absolute loser. I know that even though I never met him.

I'm distracted by something going on in the kitchen. Sandra is up and about now. She and Dad talk curtly. I want to hear, but Jasmine is going on and on about Reggie.

I give a clunky rattle to try to get her to stop.

She catches on because she too hears the sharp talk coming from the kitchen and goes silent.

"Janice saw her with him at the mall," Sandra says to Dad. "She wouldn't make that up. Give me a break, Douglas. Everyone is not against us."

"How is he not in prison?" Dad says.

"He was wearing one of those ankle bracelets. He's probably out on bond or bail or whatever you call it."

"After what he did, there is no way on earth Veronica would give him the time of day," Dad says.

"Fine, Doug. Fine. Stick your head in the sand like you always do. You're such a fool. I swear I don't know why I'm still here."

Jasmine looks at me and raises her eyebrows as she sets the electric clippers, comb, and scissors on the rolling table in preparation for my haircut.

The kitchen falls silent.

After another minute, talking resumes, but this time with my sister Veronica's voice in the mix. Dad, Sandra, and she make quiet pleasantries and Veronica says she's heading out for a class soon. She's pursuing an associate degree in land surveying at Action U (aka, The University of Akron—home of the Zips).

"Sandra says Janice Franklin saw you at the mall with Randall Bookman," Dad says. "Can you confirm that Janice was just seeing things?"

"Why are you in my business, Sandra? You're not my mom," Veronica says.

Sandra laughs defensively. "Hey, don't blame me for your poor decision-making skills. I'm just the messenger."

"Janice Franklin should mind her own business," Veronica says.

After Mom died, Veronica dated Randall Bookman, a troublemaker and black sheep. Veronica had been rebelling because she was bitter, just like Dad. She would say she'd stopped believing in God, but I know better than that.

"So, you *were* with him?" Dad says.

"Dad, please. Come on, I'm twenty and I'm smart. You don't have to worry about me. Besides, from what I overheard last night you've got enough problems of your own."

Long pause.

Jasmine and I stare at each other with our eyes and mouths gaping in anticipation.

"Who was that mobster, anyway?" Veronica says, probably referring to Sebastian.

"Don't change the subject," Dad says. "What were you doing with Randall Bookman?"

"Just talking, I swear. We walked around the mall together. That's it. We had pretzels. We didn't go anywhere. We're still friends."

"Why, though? You know he's up on robbery charges," Dad says.

"He says he's innocent."

Sandra roars with laughter. "He was caught on camera leaving that Brinks truck on his motorcycle! I can't believe they let him out."

"Five or six people did that job," Veronica says. "They all had masks on and rode common motorcycles."

"Yeah, and I've got some land to sell you in the everglades," says Sandra, followed by another guffaw.

Jasmine steps on her little stool, drapes the black hair cutting cape over my chest and, with a stretch and a sigh, hooks it around my neck.

Don't you dare turn those clippers on!

"They were all armed, Veronica," Dad insists. "He had a gun. It's armed robbery! My gosh, what are you thinking?"

Jasmine gets down from her stool and brushes off the clippers and fiddles with the guard attachments.

She wants to hear just as badly as I do.

"Please stay away from him, Veronica," Dad says. "I'm just thinking about your best interest. Your future!"

"I've got to go," Veronica says. "I'm staying on campus today. I've got another class at two."

Dad says something about breakfast, but Veronica blows it off and peaces out.

Jasmine's eyebrows bounce up and down again as she hops back up onto the stool and turns on the clippers.

5

HALE

"Oh, man, dude!" Gilbert laughs while shirking off his Army green winter coat. "Jasmine did a number on you." He stretches out the word 'you,' saying it in a funny, high-pitched tone. Then he comes over to the bed, shivers, and runs a cold hand through what's left of my hair. "It's so short! She's never taken it that low. You've got to be *freezing*."

Gilbert takes off his own gray Hurley ski cap and fits it snugly onto my head. "There." It feels good over my cold ears. I jerk and wheeze. He knows he's made me laugh.

He leans over and whispers, "Your old man keeps it cold enough in here, right? Doesn't that feel good? You can hang onto that. Maybe your dad will get the message and turn the heat up."

I flinch, then move in any way I can to let Gilbert know how much I appreciate him being here, conversing with me, treating me like a friend—like a real person.

God, it's good.

Gilbert finds the remote and turns off the TV. Then he goes over and grabs the white wooden stool he always uses, brings it right by my bed, and sits down with a huff. I always watch him like a hawk. He wears several black and brown leather bracelets on one wrist and a black Fossil watch on the other. "Speaking of your dad, he seems down, man. What's going on with him?"

I desperately want to tell him Dad's in trouble with Sebastian—

and on the rocks with Sandra. I stare at Gilbert, almost frozen, with my crippled hands jammed up beneath my chin. I try to blink but I'm not sure if I do.

Gilbert and I grew up together so we're like brothers. He lives just down the road. We went to the same school and church. When my mom died and Dad turned his back on God, Gilbert's family took Veronica, Nate, and me to church whenever we wanted to go. When it comes to walking the walk, his parents—we jokingly call them by their first names, 'Sue' and 'Fred'—are the real deal, as far as I'm concerned.

Gilbert's eyes are large and blue. He has black eyebrows and curly black hair. As usual, he's wearing skinny jeans with a thick brown leather belt that flaps around about five inches from his slender waist. He wears high-top brown leather boots and a navy V-neck sweater with a white T-shirt underneath. His limp from the bus crash is barely noticeable. Today, he looks thinner than usual, and I bet any money he's been fasting. He's done that on and off as long as I've known him—but he doesn't tell anybody.

"Cruella wasn't in a very good mood either," he whispers.

My knee-jerk laughter erupts in the form of a sudden lurch and deep groan. Gilbert knows he's struck a chord with me.

"All right Hale, my man. Let's see. Let me give you a rundown of what's going on." Gilbert looks me right in the eyes when he speaks. "I told you I'm taking classes at Action U. Getting all my core courses out of the way. That's going to take another year."

Gilbert has told me before that he hopes to transfer to Bowling Green State University, about two hours away, where the female-to-male ratio is something insane, like four females to every one guy.

I don't want him to go away. The thought of it utterly depresses me.

"I'm still working at Squeaky's. Of course, this time of year we're slow so the tips are *way* down. People only come through on the occasional clear day when they want to get all the salt and snow and scum off their cars. I may take a part-time job at the rec center at Action U to make a few more bucks."

I stare at my visitor, hoping he sees the appreciation in my eyes.

He doesn't have to come here every week. To me, that voluntary act shows he walks with God. I mean, why else would he take time out of his day to come here?

"Uh, let's see. Ellie's a senior now if you can believe that," Gilbert says, with a twinkle in his eye. "She's got guys pounding down the door, but she's not dating anyone—so you're still in the running. She wants to go to Ohio State, but Fred and Sue aren't sure we can afford it. Da-dah, da-dah, da-dah."

That last part is what Gilbert always says when me means, blah, blah, blah, or etcetera, etcetera, etcetera. I may've mentioned earlier, I'm in love with his sister, Ellie. Gilbert knows it, because it's always been that way, ever since we were little. Ellie knows it too, of course. In fact, up until my . . . undoing, I thought she may even be starting to like me.

Now, holy cow, Ellie is practically a woman. She's seventeen, a year younger than me. She came by one afternoon with Gilbert. They were dropping off a present for my birthday. It was a bird feeder that my dad has still failed to hang. It's supposed to go in the huge tree that branches out over my window. Anyway, Ellie is drop-dead gorgeous. A black-haired beauty with big dark eyes . . . you know the vintage Bob Seger tune? Her smile nukes the whole room. But, more than that, she's kind, compassionate, and so thoughtful. I've never known her to be hateful toward anyone.

She reminds me of mom.

The whole Spencer family is basically rock solid.

Best case scenario: Jesus heals me and I sweep Ellie Spencer off her feet.

Worst case scenario: well, you're pretty much looking at it.

"Hey again, Gilbert." Sandra barges into the room, looking high and low. *Probably just eavesdropping.*

"Hey, Mrs. Frodele."

"Call me Sandra. I've told you a million times."

"Okay, sure."

"I can't find my to-do list. You haven't seen a white sheet of paper . . ."

Gilbert hops up and looks around with her.

"Oh well, it's somewhere." Sandra stops searching and puts her hands on her hips. "Why do you do this, Gilbert?"

"Ma'am?"

"Come here every week."

Gilbert glances at me then turns back to her and chuckles.

"Hale's my best friend."

Sandra nods. "Yeah, right. But you don't get anything out of it. I mean, he can't . . ." She throws up her hands as if to say, "You're wasting your time, fool!"

"Oh, but I do! It's one of the most rewarding things I do. It's like the highlight of my week."

Sandra shakes her head and looks directly into my eyes.

Gilbert says, "He's in there, Sandra. He understands everything."

Chills engulf my whole body.

Preach it, bro!

She slowly turns from me, faces Gilbert, and chortles. "I'm sorry to burst your bubble, you kind soul, but the Hale we knew is gone."

Gilbert starts to protest, but she cuts him off.

"I understand you think when he *jerks* and *screeches* and *groans* and *flinches* that he's trying to communicate." Her words are exaggerated and condescending. "I thought the same thing—for about the first four to six weeks." She closes her eyes and shakes her head slowly. "I finally faced the facts. He's brain dead. Nothing more than a pitiful—"

"Stop!" Gilbert yells.

Sandra blows back two feet, her eyes and mouth gaping.

"How dare you." Gilbert lowers his voice and stands, braced like a stone wall. "What a miserable person you must be. To take your bitterness and discontentment out on him? Just because your life is dark and meaningless doesn't mean you have to take it out on Hale."

"Wait just a minute. You can't talk to me like that in my own—"

"This is *Hale's* house." He points to me with each thundering word, again, setting Cruella on her heels. "The lives these people lived before his mom died were . . . beautiful. This place was a bastion of hope and love and laughter. When she died, of course it set them back. But then you came along and basically buried them with your unbelief—"

Sandra gasps. "I'm not going to listen to this you little—"

"What's going on?" Dad enters the room with a mouthful of something, glancing at me and Gilbert, and fixing his gaze on Sandra.

She gives him a blistering look and says nothing.

"Gilbert, what happened?" Dad says.

"Nothing, Doug." Gilbert comes over to my bed and covers my hands in his briefly. Then he sits down on the stool and looks at me. "Sandra can't find her to-do list."

Red-faced Sandra curses under her breath and bolts from the room.

Dad walks over to Gilbert. "What'd she do?"

Gilbert looks at me, reaches out, and grasps my shoulder.

"This guy deserves better," Gilbert says, still looking at me.

"What'd she do?" Dad repeats.

"It's not just her." Gilbert turns and looks at my dad. "You don't believe anymore, do you?"

Dad shakes his head and sighs in exasperation. "In what? What are you talking about?"

"In God. In Hale. That he can be healed."

Dad's head rocks back and forth. "I believe Hale can be healed." He reaches over and touches my leg. But his sentiments do not seem genuine.

"By whom?" Gilbert says.

"Pardon me?"

"Who's going to heal him?"

"Okay, I'm not playing this game," Dad says.

"It's not a game, Doug. Do you still believe in God? It's a simple question." Gilbert glances at me. "Hale's listening."

6

DOUGLAS

Don't get me wrong, I genuinely love Gilbert, he's like family—but he's young and naïve—and he can be way too emotional and dramatic. Let's see how much he *believes* when he's my age, forty-seven, feeling more like seventy-five. Let's see how much he believes when his wife has been ripped from him. When his son has been killed in a church bus wreck, of all things, and the other is left a shell of the young man he was.

Let's see how much you believe then, Gilbert.

A small part of me believes Hale can understand what we are saying here by his bed. But that belief has diminished day by day for a year and is now no more than an ember in a dying fire.

"I said, I believe Hale can get well," I repeat.

"That's not what I asked you," Gilbert says. "Do you still believe in God? It's a simple question."

"Are you two done yet?" I change the subject and cross to the sink. "He's about due for lunch."

"Not yet. I brought music," Gilbert says.

"Okay." I head for the door. "How about another fifteen minutes?"

"That'll work."

I get to the door and enter the kitchen.

"Doug," Gilbert calls.

I turn back, lean against the doorframe, and look at Gilbert.

"He's in here, man. I promise you. He understands everything."

With that, Hale's body jolts as if he's just been tased, and he moans.

"You see that?" says Gilbert. "Hale needs believers around him. He needs conversation. He needs hope."

"Well, that's why you're here, right?"

I turn on my heels and stalk out of the room.

Who the heck is Gilbert Spencer to try to enlighten me about Hale's condition? He visits here once a week. I'm here 24/7, giving until I've got no more strength or sanity.

It dawns on me that Gilbert's like a grandparent. He pops onto the scene for an hour all happy and upbeat, spoils the child, gives him false hope, and leaves as quickly as he came. Leaving me with the fallout.

I'm making a peanut butter and jelly sandwich when I hear the music come on in Hale's room. Jasmine enters the kitchen carrying a laundry basket piled with clean, fresh smelling, unfolded linens.

"I think I cut his hair too short. Did you see it?" she says.

"He's got a hat on right now," I say.

"Oh shoot. See? He hates it."

"Don't worry about it. I'm sure it's fine."

"I buzzed a patch too short, then I tried to fix it and ended up taking it all down really low. Darn it."

I chuckle and offer to make Jasmine a sandwich, but she brought her own lunch, which she starts eating while folding sheets. I go to get napkins by the door to Hale's room and stop to listen to the lyrics to the song playing from a miniature Bluetooth speaker Gilbert brought with him.

I recognize the tune from the days we used to listen to that kind of music. It spoke of making a dark soul white, giving a blind man sight, and setting a shackled prisoner free.

Chills engulf me.

What feels like a tiny butterfly flutters in my stomach.

I know the words that come next—about the healing flood, the wave of grace, the tide of love . . . the healing power of Jesus' love.

Suddenly I'm shaken by a surge of emotion—about my failure as a father, my bitterness toward God, and Gilbert's unflinching hope and undying friendship. About the threatening predicament with Sebastian. If only Cindy were here—we could get through this together. But no. Instead, I spurn God and marry someone I should have known would bring out the worst in me.

"Doug!" Jasmine laughs with a humorous and exaggerated look of shock on her face.

I wipe a tear from my eye and turn to her. "Sorry. What?"

"What is with you?" she says.

"Nothing. Nothing."

"You were just in la la land, I swear. What's going on?"

I muster a snicker and go back to my sandwich. "Just tired."

"I've heard that one before."

My phone buzzes in my pocket. At the same time, Sandra breezes into the kitchen wearing her navy winter coat and gray stocking cap, which looks ridiculous.

A glance at my phone shows it's Assistant Pastor Rick Powers calling again.

"There's too much commotion around here," Sandra says, grabbing her purse and keys. "I'm going to the library to work. Don't wait on me for dinner. There's frozen pizza and TV dinners."

Lovely.

I wonder whether Sandra has eaten lunch, but then have the merciless thought that she never misses a meal.

I truly am turning into a grouchy old man.

My phone continues to vibrate. This guy isn't giving up until he reaches me.

I shoot Sandra a fake smile and answer the call.

"Hey, this is Doug."

"Doug Frodele! Man, it's good to hear your voice."

"Hey, Rick. It's been a long time." Three years to be precise, since Cindy died, since I left the fold at Crossroads Community Church.

"I'm sorry to keep bugging you, but when I saw you'd called I couldn't wait to talk. What's going on? What can I do for you?"

It crosses my mind to not do this, to figure something else out, but the clock is ticking and I have only until tomorrow night to repay Sebastian. I have to get into that church.

"I was wondering if I could come see you—at the church."

"Well, certainly. I'd love that. Pastor Brent will be thrilled to see you, too. Everybody will."

"Uh, listen, if you don't mind, Rick, let's keep it on the DL. I just want this to be between us. I just need a . . . a friend to confide in right now. In fact, is there any chance we could do it today? This afternoon?"

"Oh gosh, Doug. Let's see . . ."

As Rick pauses, the pressure mounts in my chest, knowing I have only about thirty-six hours to get the money or something very bad is going to happen. "I'll only keep you thirty minutes," I say. "I just need someone to talk to and you keep coming to my mind. I'm kind of desperate."

The truth is, Rick is the most gullible person I can think of at Crossroads, plus, the safe is in his office—at least it used to be.

"Well, okay," Rick says. "I can make it work if you can be here by one. Is that possible? One-fifteen at latest? I'll just eat lunch while we talk. That way I can still keep my afternoon appointments."

I look at my watch and my heart rate kicks up a notch. That gives me forty minutes to get to the church, plenty of time.

"That'll be perfect, Rick. Thank you so much. I'll look forward to seeing you."

Rick goes on and on about how excited he is that I've reached out to the church again.

Little does the man know that the only reason I'm reaching out to the beloved church is to see if the safe is still in the same place, if the combination could possibly still be the same, and if they still wait to make their once-a-month bank deposit until the fifteenth of each month—which is one week away.

As we agree to see each other soon and hang up, I race downstairs to my workshop in the basement to make sure I still have my key to the church and the stamp I always used as an elder to endorse the tithe checks each month.

It'll be just like old times, only this time, there will be something in it for me.

7

HALE

I'd never heard the song Gilbert played for me because it was about twenty years old, but it stirred my soul to the core and made me wheeze uncontrollably. It gave me *hope*. Gilbert said he found the song while going through his dad's playlist. I wish he would leave it here and let it play around the clock, instead of the blasted TV.

"Okay, I need to get going, but there's one last thing I want to share with you before I take off," Gilbert says as he sits perched on the white stool right next to me.

"Hey boys." Dad breezes into the room wearing his heavy coat and black ski cap. "I've got to go meet somebody so Jasmine's going to feed you, Hale. You about done, Gilbert?"

"Five more minutes and I'm gone."

"That'll work," Dad says. "Thanks for coming. You're a good friend."

"You're welcome. By the way, Doug, I didn't mean any offense to you—earlier. Sorry about that."

Dad comes over and stands next to Gilbert and looks him in the eyes. "We're all on our own journeys, Gilbert. I don't expect you to understand where I am, and vice versa. Regardless of any differences, we truly appreciate you coming here each week. It's admirable and I know Hale loves it more than anything."

My body jolts and freezes up like a marble statue. I hear myself moan. It sounds incredibly painful, but it's the only way I can agree with Dad about how much I love Gilbert's visits.

"Whoa. Take it easy there, big guy." Gilbert rests a hand on my shoulder, then looks at Dad. "I'm afraid I overstepped my boundaries with Sandra. I said some things I shouldn't have. I feel bad about it."

Doug shrugs and sighs. "It is what it is." He turns and walks toward the door. "Maybe they were things she needed to hear."

Yeah, and maybe the things Gilbert said to you were things you need to hear!

Dad is gone and it's just us again.

"Man," Gilbert says softly. "I never lose my temper like that. That wasn't cool."

I want to tell him Sandra needed to hear it. Dad too!

I grunt, trying to tell him it's all okay.

"I know—you would've handled it a lot better than I did," he says. "Okay, listen, over the weekend I did some reading." Gilbert leans to one side and takes a piece of paper out of his back pocket and unfolds it. "It made me think of you. Two simple things. One, remember Jairus? He begs for Jesus to come to his house because his twelve-year-old daughter is dying. So, they head for his house. But on the way, a woman who's had chronic bleeding for twelve years—that nobody could heal—touches the fringe of Jesus's robe and her bleeding stops instantly."

Gilbert makes a funny expression, eyes huge, head craned back.

Inside, I'm laughing my buns off and am beyond excited about the story, about someone sitting here conversing with me as if I'm a real human being.

Gilbert looks at his notes again.

"Jesus says, 'Who touched me?' The disciples go, 'Bro, the whole crowd is pressing in on you. Everyone's touching you.' But Jesus says, 'I felt *power* leave me.'" Gilbert glimpses at me as if he's telling a child an exciting bedtime story. "So, the woman freaks out, falls at his feet, trembling, and admits she touched him in order to get healed."

Gilbert looks at me, leans in close, and says, "You know what Jesus said to her?" Long pause. "He said, 'Daughter, your *faith* has made you well.'"

I want to bolt upright. Reach up to the sky. Touch his robe myself. I feel my face go red hot. I'm making some idiotic sound that's plain embarrassing.

Gilbert nods and whispers, "Your faith in him can make you well, bro."

He waits for me to calm down.

"Here's the killer part. While Jesus is still talking to the lady, someone runs up and says to Jairus, 'Hey, your daughter has died. There's no need to trouble Jesus anymore.'"

Gilbert cranes his neck toward me, staring into my eyes with drama. And he whispers, "This next part is what I want you to remember." He looks at the piece of paper. He reads slowly, exaggeratedly, and with passion. "When Jesus heard the girl was dead, he looks at Jairus and says, 'Do not be afraid any longer—*only believe.*'"

Gilbert stops reading, looks at me, and leans back on the stool. "Only believe. Nothing else. Clear your mind of any worry, fear, or doubt. *Only believe.*"

I'm crying now, but it's sounding more like someone just chopped off one of my fingers.

"I know!" Gilbert nods. "I know, bro. It's powerful. The daughter was basically dead. But what? Don't be afraid—only believe. And to the woman he said, 'Your *faith* has made you well.' Let's both meditate on that this week."

Gilbert gets up and sweeps the stool back where it belongs and crosses back over to me. "I've got to roll, bro. I'm going to let you hang onto that hat until next time, okay? Maybe your dad will get the hint and turn the heat up."

My back arches and I lament.

He starts getting his coat on.

"Okay, boys, it's past feeding time." Jasmine breezes into the room, all business, carrying a package of my food and setting up the pump.

I sigh knowing it will be another week before I see Gilbert again.

He comes back over, leans in close, and whispers, "I gave you one job: *only believe.*"

8

DOUGLAS

As I swing into one of the plowed parking spaces at Crossroads Community Church in Akron, I'm taken aback by how much the grounds have changed and the buildings have improved in the three years since I've been here. Hale had mentioned, before his accident, about the changes that had been in progress, but I guess I'd only half-listened.

There's a beautiful large new structure at the south end of the complex, which I figure houses the new classrooms and youth sanctuary we'd long planned. The parking lot has doubled in size and, although most of it is blanketed in snow, I can see where they've plowed that it's been newly black-topped and painted with crisp, bright white lines. Professional landscaping has been done all around the buildings where I see new trees, shrubs, and lighting.

The money is definitely rolling in.

Twelve to fifteen cars dot the parking lot, telling me the staff has grown exponentially since I've been here.

I'm hopeful there's plenty of money in the coffers, but with all the growth and changes, I'm doubtful the old safe and system are still in place. If I luck out and they are the same, I can come back at night, get what's in the safe, endorse the checks and say the cash is going to the Akron Homeless Shelter, which is, or was, one of the church's main charity recipients. Even if Pastor Rick figures out it's me, he'll have no evidence.

As I grab my keys and phone, lock the car, and head toward the main entrance, I'm hoping I don't see anyone I know, especially the head pastor, Brent Miller. Although he was gracious when I left, I'm still somewhat embarrassed to show my face around here.

Oh look, it's Douglas Frodele, whose faith failed when tragedy struck, and who's become a backslidden unbeliever.

It is a frigid, gray day. As I crunch through the salt on the steps and approach the front door my heart sinks. They've installed a small security camera up high above the doors. There are probably more inside.

I suppose I could wear some sort of mask, but as the reality of this outlandish caper sinks in I'm thinking there's no way I can pull it off.

In fact it's idiotic.

Part of me wants to turn and leave, but I'm desperate.

Play it out and see what happens. You have nothing to lose.

The shiny floors are new and the whole place has been professionally painted. A blond receptionist whom I gladly don't recognize greets me and I tell her I'm here to see Pastor Rick. But at that very moment, he turns a corner, blurts out my name, and gives me a hug.

"I saw you pull in." His smile tells me he's genuinely glad to see me. He shakes my hand and pats my shoulder. "Come on back. Your timing is perfect. I'm just having a quick bite."

"My gosh, you've lost weight," I say. "You look great."

He laughs as we walk down the bright hallway I remember so well.

"Believe it or not, Carrie and I made a new year's resolution—together. She's lost twenty-four pounds and I've lost twenty-nine. We both have more to go."

Rick is about thirty-five-years old. He's tall, with a full head of hair the color of his khaki pants. He wears a blue oxford shirt with a navy sweater, and Sperrys. The weight loss is obvious in his face, neck, and his entire frame.

"Wow. Congratulations," I say, glad we are headed in the exact direction of his old office, but not glad to see another camera up high to the right. "How did you do it? Diet? Exercise?"

"Both, actually. We're walking together in the evenings, which has been really tough with the winter we've had." We both laugh as he turns left into his same old office! "And we're just eating better. Nothing unrealistic. We've just cut back on things like pasta, bread, red meat—"

"All the good stuff."

We both laugh again, and I realize I better get serious if there's any chance he's going to buy my sob story.

"Have a seat." He points to my choice of two chairs, then goes around and sits behind his desk. "I hope you don't mind if I eat while we talk."

"Of course not."

In front of him sits an enormous clear water bottle, half full, and a massive salad in a plastic container—leaf lettuce, carrots, red onion, egg. "Let me pray for us real quick," he says.

Those words sound foreign and weird to me after three years away from Christian circles.

After he says a fast prayer—including a shout out for my well-being—he spreads a paper towel in his lap and dives in, using real silverware.

"Tell me what's new," he says with a mouthful. "Or start wherever you want. I'm just so glad to see you. You were such a vital part of this place."

There is another tiny camera mounted behind him, above his head to the left, which causes a trickle of sweat to arise on my forehead.

I look down at my lap, both for dramatic affect and to seriously get my mind focused on what I've planned to say.

I look up into his brown eyes. "We've hit hard times, Rick."

He pauses, then nods slightly as he chews—waiting for more.

"The expenses for Hale have been . . . out of sight. We're still in debt for the medical bills, plus we've had to buy all kinds of expensive equipment, meds, special food. We had Nathaniel's funeral expenses. It's just been major. Heck, Veronica's paying for her own college, which Cindy and I never intended."

All of that is true, of course.

Rick shakes his head and wipes his mouth with his napkin. "I'm so sorry, Doug. I can't imagine having all that financial pressure, on top of the grief of losing Cindy and Nate—"

"And Hale, really. I mean, he's . . . he requires twenty-four-seven care. He's fed with a g-tube." I find myself getting choked up. "We have a part-time nurse—"

"Another expense."

"Yes. We'd have full-time care, but there's no way we can pay for that."

Rick rakes and jabs at the salad, taking another enormous bite. "Now, I know you lost your job back when . . . after Cindy passed. Are you working?"

"I'm a postal carrier with the USPS. I'm off today. It doesn't pay much, but it's what I could find; the benefits are good. Our debt is the problem. It's killing us."

He nods exaggeratedly, probably thinking I'm a lazy low life only looking for a handout.

"And I heard you remarried . . ."

Oh, here come all the questions to see whether I check all the Christian boxes.

I nod. "Sandra. Yep. She does medical transcription."

"I see." He pauses, perhaps expecting me to say more about Sandra.

But I'm not going there.

"Tell me how things are—spiritually. What's going on?" Rick says.

The dreaded question. I knew something like this was coming. He's obligated to ask this stuff.

"Not good. It's been a lot to overcome."

"I can only imagine. Are you going to church anywhere?"

I shake my head curtly. "No."

It dawns on me that, so far, I've told the complete truth. I've not lied to him. Who knows, if I stay the course, maybe he'll help bail us out.

Rick sets the silverware in the unfinished salad and slides it away. He wipes his mouth, clears his throat, and leans back in his chair. "Tell me what I can do for you, Doug. Why did you think of me, and why are you here?"

I clear my own throat and lean forward resting my arms on my knees. "I know we used to have a Benevolence Fund..."

Rick rocks back and tents his hands at his mouth. His eyes shift from me to where the safe used to be, to the doorway.

"Really, too, I just wanted to get your counsel," I say, venturing into lying territory, trying to stroke his ego enough to make something good happen.

"How much do you need?" Rick says. "I'm only asking; I'm not promising anything. Please understand that."

I wince and tell him thirty thousand.

He flinches and his eyes widen.

I hear footsteps in the hallway and turn just in time to make eye contact with Pastor Brent Miller. For a split-second, I believe we both recognize each other, even though he's grown a beard, and we both look away. He continues walking.

"That was Brent," Rick says. "You want to say hey?"

"No, Rick, I really don't. I'm... no, thanks."

"I understand." He nods and leans forward, gripping the arms of his chair, but freezing there, as if deep in thought.

My hunch is that he may go ask Brent if he can give me some money from the Benevolence Fund.

If he leaves the room, I'm going to check and see if the safe is in the same place, behind his credenza—just five to six feet away.

"You know what, Doug," Rick stands, "I'll be right back. I'm going to check on something really quickly."

"Sure. Take your time."

9

DOUGLAS

The second Rick is out of sight, I take a deep breath and quietly dash over to the long, dark wooden credenza and lean against the wall to see if the safe is still back there. It used to be built right into the wall, down low, bolted to the wood studs behind the drywall. A web of cords from a printer, scanner, lamp, and who knows what else, prevent me from spotting the safe.

I stand still there for a moment, my heart racing as I stare at the doorway and listen for Rick.

Seeing and hearing nothing, I hurry to the other end of the credenza and attempt to push it a few inches away from the wall so I can see back in there. But the credenza doesn't budge; it weighs a ton. My forehead sweats. I crouch low to get better leverage. I listen for footsteps. Hearing nothing, I push as hard as I can. To my surprise, and horror, the credenza jerks four inches from the wall and the tall glass lamp teeters.

Two thoughts fast-forward through my mind: *one, I see that the safe is still back there; two, the lamp is going to crash and break.*

I lurch for it and snatch it awkwardly just as it's headed off the edge toward the floor. I mangle it clumsily, almost dropping it.

But I have it.

I stand frozen, clutching the lamp.

I can barely breathe.

Male voices are coming in the hallway.

I bang the lamp back down and, with all the weight I can muster, use my thighs to shove the credenza back against the wall. The lamp wobbles violently again, but I steady it. I notice the credenza is not fully back in place, but the approaching voices beckon me to race back to my chair in a huff.

Sweat covers my face.

Pastor Brent enters first with his hand outstretched. "My goodness, Douglas Frodele, how good to see you. I thought you looked familiar when I passed earlier."

You knew it was me.

Rick quietly follows Brent into the office. His head is down, and he wears a slight smile, as if he's saving the day by ushering in the king.

I stand, wipe the sweat from my face onto my pants, and shake Brent's hand, hoping he doesn't feel the dampness.

I feel visibly shaken, but manage to say, "Brent, good to see you."

Rick glances at the lamp, tilts his head at the credenza, then looks at me curiously.

I swallow hard thinking he can't possibly notice it's been moved.

Brent squints at me and forces a smile. He detects my uneasiness.

"Rick tells me you're in a difficult place." The senior pastor is under six-feet tall, has a barrel chest, and wears brown slacks, a white shirt, and a brown tie. He is about forty-five, a bit overweight, with curly dark hair that's grayed immensely in three years; the beard is fully gray. "Shall we sit for a minute?"

I hesitate.

These men used to be my best friends.

"I really didn't want to get you involved," I say, glancing at Rick with the slightest look of irritation.

Pastor Brent purses his lips and sits down in one of the two chairs and waves a hand for me to take the other. Following his cue, Rick walks around his desk and sits in his chair.

"Sit down for a minute, Doug," Brent insists.

I do so.

"Tell me how you are."

Oh brother. Here we go again.

Now I truly feel like the backslidden black sheep—with the two shepherds trying to herd me back into the fold.

"Brent, to be honest, I shared with Rick and really just wanted this to be between—"

"He told me a little."

Frustrated, I say, "I really didn't want him to."

"Well, he said you mentioned the Benevolence Fund," Brent says a bit sternly. "Rick's just trying to help. Anything that comes out of there goes through me, first. So . . ."

My face is hot with anger and humiliation, and I can only nod and wipe more sweat away.

What was I thinking coming here in the first place?

"Can you tell me, if we were to give you some funds, what you would do with it?"

Oh sure, Pastor, I'll be using it to pay off a mobster named Sebastian—before he slits my throat.

Rick picks at his salad and glances at his watch.

I guess I need to play their game. "We have a lot of medical debt—from Hale's accident. I'm behind on payments. Way behind."

Brent presses his index fingers together in the shape of a church steeple against his mouth and stares at me.

Rick has lost interest in his salad and is examining the credenza—and the lamp.

I look that way too and see that the credenza is slightly crooked.

He knows I know the safe is back there.

"If it's not too personal a question, may I ask how much debt you have?" Brent says.

Rick has now mentally dropped out of the conversation and is moving his computer mouse, tapping the keyboard, and looking at his screen, which faces him only.

"A lot," I say, growing uneasy about whatever is fascinating Rick so much on his computer. "The lion's share of our income now goes toward making payments on our debt."

"I see," Brent says. "I am sorry you're having such a difficult time." He looks over at Rick, whose shoulders have become erect and whose face is just twelve inches from his glowing computer screen. "Rick?"

Rick continues staring wide-eyed at the screen for five more seconds, then looks at Brent, but his eyes shift to me with a slow blink and a somber frown.

"What do you say?" Brent says. "Can we help Doug out with a payment or two?"

But—something is wrong.

Rick knows . . . *he knows what I did.*

Rick clears his throat, grimaces, interlocks his fingers, and rests his hands on his desk.

"We could do that," Rick says with a pause. "What's changed since you were here, Doug, is that most people give to the church online now, so we keep very little money in the old safe." His words are sharp and condemning.

Brent squints at Rick with a questioning face and sets his shoulders back. "I meant, just write him a check."

Rick nods. "Right. Okay. We'll take care of that." Rick stands as if to end the meeting.

Brent stands and reaches his hand out to me.

I shake his hand and stand, too.

"God bless you, Doug," Brent says. "I hope things look up for you." He nods toward Rick. "I hope this will help a little bit."

"I'm sure it will. Thank you, Brent."

"We'd love to see you and your family back here someday."

I watch him leave the room and I continue staring at the doorway after he's out of sight, holding my breath for fear of what's to come when I turn back to Rick.

I muster the courage and turn to look at him.

With a grunt, Rick lifts the large computer screen, turns it around toward me, and plunks it down.

On the screen is a large rectangular box with a frozen video frame. It's me, five minutes ago, kneeling at the end of the credenza when they were out of the room.

Rick just stares at me with his lips sealed and a look of hurt in his eyes.

My head drops in disgust.

The image of what I've become is seared in my mind.

"This is low, Doug."

I shake my head and look up at him, fighting back tears.

"I'm going to keep this between us," he says.
As I say thank you, a cry spills out with it.
Rick walks over to me, stops, and holds his arms out.
I hug him. He hugs me.
We stay like that for maybe five seconds.
I turn and rush out, unable to look at his face again.

10

HALE

It's mid-afternoon and I'm strapped onto the medical tilt table, standing straight up-and-down at a ninety-degree angle, just like a normal human being. *Well, not quite.* If Jasmine undid the three massive, ten-inch-wide bands that are tight against my chest, waist, and knees, I would collapse like an imploding skyscraper.

"Try to keep your head up," she says. "If you don't, I'm going to have to strap it back, and you always hate me for that."

I want to do what she says.

My head rolls toward my chest, then back up and around. I try with all my *guts* to keep it up—but there's a disconnect.

As usual, Jasmine's got me in a white gown and wearing knee-high royal blue compression socks. *If Ellie Spencer saw me now, that would be the end of it.* My feet rest on the base of the tilt table. The thing is on wheels, it's electric, and it probably cost twenty grand.

"Hale, I'm going to get your arms out for a little bit so you can stretch," says Jasmine, hopping up onto the base of the unit. *I love it when she does this.* It's not easy for her, because she's so tiny. She's so close I can smell her lotion and a hint of perfume. She shoves all her upper weight into my chest and loosens the top strap, freeing my left arm first, then my right. Then she hops down and tightens the top band with a grunt.

With that, I let out a joyful reaction that sounds like an old man snoring loudly.

"I know you like that." She comes along my left side and tries to straighten my rigid arm and hand. She gently rolls it in ways it seldom moves. Again, I groan from the pain and pleasure of it.

"So what, you don't like your haircut? You still got that hat on. I'm going to let that Gilbert have it the next time I see him."

I moan, trying to tell her not to take the hat off.

"You want it off?"

No!

Jasmine steps onto the base of the tilt table with a squeak, stretches up, and removes the hat. Her face glistens with sweat.

My upper body jolts. I hear myself let out a long and sorrowful wail.

"Okay, okay! My goodness..." She stretches on her tiptoes with her tongue sticking out like Michael Jordan and puts the ski cap back on my head. It feels crooked, but at least she got the message.

She hops down. "My land, Hale Frodele, you can be one Grumpy Gus. Have I ever told you that before? I'm going to start calling you Gus."

I give a belly laugh that comes out sounding like I've been stabbed.

Jasmine laughs too as she starts doing my right arm.

"Darn. I forgot to trim your eyebrows. They are a hot mess. Remind me to do that, okay? You look like an old man."

My eyebrows.

I was in about fifth grade when I first really noticed or cared about the fact that my eyebrows were pointy, each shaped like the top of a pyramid. We'd received our school photos that day, and I was horrified. My cartoon-like eyebrows made me look hyper alert—all the time.

I hear a car in the driveway but can't see it because I'm turned into the room away from the window.

Jasmine doesn't notice.

Anyway, I rushed home with my school pictures that day and found my mom. "Mom, do my eyebrows look funny?" She must have known what I meant. I'll never forget her kind, pretty face as she slowly looked through the pictures and drew close to me.

"Do they look weird?" I said. "They point up in the middle."

With her beautiful face close to mine, she said, "Hale Frodele, you are the cutest, most distinct-looking, most *handsome* young man I do believe I have ever seen."

I always believed her.

God, I wish she was here now.

She would believe.

She would pull us through.

She would pray for a miracle—until we got one.

A door slams in the house.

Jasmine hears it, gives me a questioning glance, and heads inside. Soon I hear talking.

It's Sandra. Back early from the library.

I don't think she ever went in the first place. I think she went someplace else.

"Where's Douglas?" Sandra says.

I hear Jasmine's voice, probably explaining he ran out to meet someone.

Sandra curses, says it's critical she speak to him, then pounds up the stairs.

"Whew, boy." Jasmine blows back into my room. "Your stepmom's in a tizzy. Why doesn't she just call him if she's got to talk to him so bad?"

She jabs a button and the tilt table begins to recline with a soft buzzing noise, steadily sending me back to the horizontal position.

"Sorry, bud. I'm going to get you back into the bed. It feels like some fireworks about to go down at the Frodele residence."

When the table is finally flat and I'm staring straight up at the white ceiling, Jasmine leans over and pushes it with all her might, rolling me over toward the bed. But I'm not aligned side-by-side like I need to be.

"Shoot." She sighs and arches her back. "Your dad usually helps me with this. It's so dang awkward."

She wheels me several feet backward . . . forward . . . backward. "I swear they don't pay me enough."

Finally, I come in for a bumpy landing snug against my bed.

Jasmine huffs and wipes her forehead.

"I need help getting you over," she whispers.

Yes, please!

She once tried to roll me from the table into the bed by herself and, even though she had all the wheels locked, I ended up getting sucked into the crack like a mannequin in quicksand.

Noises come from the kitchen.

Jasmine goes inside again.

I hear her ask whoever it is if they can help get me into my bed.

It's Sandra, who gives her some backtalk. But Jasmine stands up to her and insists she can't do it alone.

"Fine, let's get it over with," Sandra says. "I've got things to do."

They enter my room, Sandra leading the way.

"What's he doing with that stupid hat on?" She rips it off my head.

I convulse.

My face goes, *woosh*, like a blazing inferno.

"Whoa, I think he wants that on," Jasmine says.

Sandra tosses the hat onto the counter by the sink, looks at me, and says, "Wow! You think you could cut his hair any shorter? He looks like a . . ."

"I made a mistake, okay? My gosh, Sandra." Jasmine crosses to the counter, snatches the hat, comes over, puts it back on my head, and pats it for good measure.

Good for you! I love you, Jasmine!

Sandra chuckles in a sarcastic tone. "I think you forgot his eyebrows—they're longer than his hair." She cackles at her own joke.

"Thanks for reminding me." Jasmine goes over, opens a low cupboard, and searches in her box of hair stuff. "Where are my scissors?" She bangs the cupboard closed and stalks into the house.

"Hey," Sandra yells at Jasmine, "let's get this done. You can do that later."

Sandra approaches me. She's just pumped a glob of lotion into her hands from my lotion bottle by the window and is rubbing her hands together. She stops right next to the bed and looks down at me while working the lotion into her wrists and hands.

"You think your dad hung the moon, don't you?" she says quietly. "Do you understand he borrowed thirty thousand dollars from Sebastian? Well, twenty, actually, plus ten in interest. How's he gonna repay that in," she looks at her watch, "thirty hours?" She frowns and shakes her head. "Your dad could have weathered your mom's death. We were on our way. And he could have survived Nathaniel's death." She looks toward the door to make sure Jasmine isn't nearby, then back at me with clenched teeth. "But you, young man, will be your father's *demise*."

I can only stare at her with watery eyes and a gaping mouth. I don't have the spirit or fortitude or vocabulary or energy to protest. In fact, she's probably right.

How long can I expect Dad to do this with me? Am I going to be here in this bed when I'm thirty? Forty? What about when Dad's gone? Who's going to get stuck with me then, Veronica? The state of Ohio?

"Where are my scissors?" Jasmine yells in frustration from somewhere in the house.

Sandra bends over close to me.

"The way I see it," she whispers, "there's only one way for me to save my marriage, save this house, and salvage a decent life." She rests a hand on my head, stares at me, tilts her head, then snatches the hat off my head. "And that's if you're out of the picture."

11

HALE

I awaken. It's dark outside my window. I must have dozed off. What is this, Tuesday? *Yeah, Tuesday.* Dead of winter in the Rust Belt—pitch black at 4:15 p.m.

Oh, man.

I remember the throwdown with Sandra.

What *was* that?

My body locks up.

Did she actually threaten me? What did she say? The only way she can save her marriage and the house is if I'm 'out of the picture?'

I hear myself murmur.

I feel trapped . . . *trapped in here!*

This is on Dad.

He's blind!

He has no clue what kind of person Sandra really is.

Plus, we've got the whole deal with Sebastian—the thirty grand is due tomorrow.

Someone needs to *do* something.

Uh-oh, uh-oh.

I'm thrashing . . . losing it.

"Whoa, whoa, whoa." Dad calls as he rushes into my room. "It's okay, it's okay, Hale."

His hands are on me.

I'm writhing.

51

He's trying to hold me down with a sad, scared look in his eyes . . . forcing a smile through gritted teeth, forcing me down.

"Everything's fine, buddy. Calm down. Calm down. Relax. Just relax."

I give one last flinch and go limp.

He grabs the cloth from the bed rail and wipes the sweat from my forehead, then my mouth.

"Cool down, cool down."

He finishes mopping off my face and neck and upper chest, and I finally lay back all the way.

"You haven't done that in a long time, pal. What's going on?"

"What happened?" Veronica enters the room nonchalantly, peeling a cheese stick, tilting her head back, and eating a few strings at a time.

"Not sure," Dad says. "He was super agitated."

"It's probably shopping channel overload. Look at this . . ."

We all look at the blasted TV, which is showing an overweight, middle-aged man munching popcorn in his recliner while wearing the clearance item of the day: sauna pants.

Veronica finds the remote, jabs it toward the screen, and the TV goes black.

Finally.

"Crap. What happened to his hair?" she says, tossing the remote onto my bed.

It must really be bad.

"Jasmine said she made a mistake, then tried to correct it," Dad says.

"Wow, he needs lotion." Veronica pops the end of the cheese stick in her mouth, comes over, pumps some lotion, rubs it in her hands, then gently covers my hands in hers and begins to massage it in.

"How were classes?" Dad says.

"Not bad. The one professor is a loser. We basically teach ourselves from the book. He does online classes half the time."

Veronica puts down the rail on her side and sits on my bed, gently rubbing the lotion into my rigid hands and arms.

I AM IN HERE

Dad asks more about her classes and they chat for a minute. A concise exchange, but at least they're talking.

That's what I want—for everyone to just get along.

"So, are you gonna tell me who that guy was, last night?" she says.

Oh, this'll be interesting.

Dad sighs and looks out the window.

"He looked like one of the guys from The Sopranos," she adds.

"His name is Sebastian," Dad says, still staring into the dark. "Sandra introduced me to him. I had to borrow money . . . to keep up with the bills."

"You borrowed money from that guy? What's wrong with the bank?"

"We maxed out all our bank loans."

"How much—did you borrow?"

Dad turns and looks at Veronica soberly. "Twenty thousand, plus ten thousand interest."

Veronica stops rubbing my hands. Her brown eyes grow huge, her mouth drops open, and her skinny neck cranes toward Dad.

He shrugs. "It is what it is."

"I take it he wants his money. Is that what he was doing here?"

Dad nods. "It's been due for three weeks. We don't have it."

Veronica cusses in awe.

"Please don't do that," Dad says. "Since when do we use that kind of language around here?"

"Sorry. So, what happens now?"

"Supposedly, I have until tomorrow night."

"Tomorrow night! Then what?"

He shakes his head and takes another deep breath and sighs. "I don't know."

"Will he come back here? Will he try to hurt you? What the heck, Dad? Are we in danger?" Veronica stands and locks my railing back in place. She uses the cloth on the rail to wipe her hands, tosses it, then stares at Dad with her fists on her hips, biting her bottom lip.

This is the most I've seen her care about family matters in months.

He looks at her as if in a trance and says nothing.

"Dad, wake up!" She snaps her fingers several times. "My gosh.

We could all be in danger. What are you going to do about it? It's like you don't even care. Do you at least have a gun in the house?"

The word 'gun' makes him flinch slightly, as if waking him from a daydream, but he continues to stare at her with a glazed look in his eyes.

"Ever since Mom died, you've been like this. You're like a zombie. You need to snap out of it. You've still got a family. We may be a bunch of broken rejects, but you're stuck with us."

Hey, speak for yourself sister!

"Oh, dear. What's all this about?" Sandra comes sauntering in carrying an icy adult beverage in a tall glass. I can smell the booze from my bed.

Dad's and Veronica's heads turn to Sandra at the same time, then they look away. Neither of them say a word.

Sandra looks at Dad and says, "Did you tell her?"

"Is this guy dangerous?" Veronica says to Sandra. "Dad says you introduced him. Where do you know him from?"

Sandra raises her eyebrows. She sneezes, walks over, grabs a tissue, wipes her nose, and stuffs the tissue in her pocket.

"I guess your dad should have asked those questions before he borrowed thirty grand from the man."

"Why don't you answer her question?" Dad says.

Sandra sets her shoulders back as if bored. "We go way back. Knew each other during high school. Had mutual friends. I don't know him that well. But, when I asked around, I was told he could come up with a loan."

"What's going to happen if we can't pay it back by tomorrow—which we can't?" Veronica says.

Sandra chuckles. "Well, your dear old dad is going to figure that one out, aren't you Douglas?"

Dad looks from Sandra, to Veronica, to me—but says nothing.

"I can tell you this much," Sandra says, "if we can't pay, it's not going to be pretty what happens tomorrow night. Sebastian doesn't run with the best crowd. He wasn't lying, it probably won't be him that shows up."

"Why would you refer him to my dad—if he's that bad?" Veronica says. "You've been nothing but a destructive—"

"Hey! Your dad was desperate. Tell her, Doug! You practically begged me to help you find a loan." She cusses and jabs a finger at Dad. "This is why she and I don't get along, because you're always portraying me as the bad guy."

"Isn't there anything you can do—since you're friends with Sebastian?" Veronica says to Sandra.

Sandra's eyes bulge and she nods emphatically. "What do you think I've been doing for the last three weeks? I'm the one who's been stalling him. If it wasn't for me . . . well, who knows what would've happened by now."

Sandra takes a sloppy swig of her drink and wipes her mouth with the back of her free hand. "I'll tell you this much, I won't be around for the fireworks tomorrow night." She points to Veronica with the glass in her hand. "I suggest you don't be here either."

I hear something outside.

A car coming up the driveway.

I try to look, but I'm faced the other way and can't make myself roll over to the window.

No one else notices.

"Where do you think you're going to go?" Dad says.

Sandra shrugs. "Anywhere but here. Hotel. Airbnb. Anyplace."

I hear a phone vibrate.

Dad tells Veronica she should plan to go with Sandra as he digs his phone out of his back pocket, examines the screen, and looks up at the girls.

"It's Gilbert. He's here. He wants to see Hale."

12

DOUGLAS

Veronica has turned on the charm, given Gilbert a hug, and ushered him into Hale's room. They are talking quietly just inside the doorway, about classes and old acquaintances, as Hale watches intently from his bed with his mouth open wide. Veronica, Hale, and Nathaniel grew up with Gilbert and his sister, Ellie Spencer, so they are like family. They live just down the road. Our families went to church together, did everything together.

Sandra disappeared into the house without greeting Gilbert. She's probably stationed herself in front of the TV in our bedroom with her drink, which she topped off with Vodka in the kitchen before exiting, and a colossal bag of pretzels, which she grabbed from the pantry on her way upstairs.

I'm washing Hale's face with a hot washcloth to refresh him and will feed him after Gilbert leaves. Hale is craning his neck toward the door; he can't take his eyes off Gilbert, who rarely comes to the house this late in the day, especially unannounced.

As Gilbert and Veronica reminisce, I recall thinking on more than one occasion in the distant past that perhaps those two may someday end up together, even though Veronica is several years older. And that Hale may end up with Ellie, whom he's loved ever since they were kids.

Those naïve hopes are long gone now.

I was living in a bubble . . . a Christian bubble.

In my naivety, I thought if I lived in ways that pleased God, he would bless me in return. All would be well. Isn't that what the Bible states in a million different ways and places? That, if we are good Christians, if we obey his commands, we will be healthy, wealthy, and wise; we will be protected, upheld, and favored?

That charade got blown to smithereens the day Cindy was diagnosed. And then she died. And two years later we lost Nate. And I've been in a dark, dark place ever since.

I had mistakenly viewed God as the great cosmic vending machine. If I am faithful to do A, God rewards me with B.

I found out the hard way that is not the way life works.

Hale moans in a low, deep tone, cocking his neck, wanting to be part of the conversation between Gilbert and Veronica.

"Just relax, buddy," I whisper. "They're talking. Let them talk, okay? Veronica needs that."

It's dark outside and I notice my reflection in the window. I'm hunched over like an old man, so I set my shoulders back. I've pretty much quit caring what I look like and realize I've aged ten years in the last three.

I run a finger along Hale's pointy eyebrows, realizing Jasmine must have trimmed them. I think she shaved him, too. His skin is white. His cheeks are red with chafe from the winter.

Gilbert shrugs off his coat and hangs it on a hook on the coat rack.

They are talking intently in an upbeat tone and seem to be enjoying catching up. Veronica offers him hot cocoa and they head into the kitchen.

Now alone in the room with Hale, I am suddenly embarrassed all over again by the memory of Pastor Rick catching me on video scoping out the safe in his office. I wonder if he told Pastor Brent after all?

How low can you get?

I'm certain that they and many others think of me as the once-on-fire-Christian, now-backslidden-lowlife scum of the earth.

Let them think what they want . . . who cares?

See how they respond when their young wives and sons are taken from them.

I can only draw two possible conclusions from the cruel, heartbreaking misery that's happened over the last three years. One is that God doesn't exist, the Bible is a myth, and there is no heaven or hell.

But I lean toward the second, that God does exist, and he is coldly incomprehensible. I've thought about the book of Job a lot since Cindy and Nate died, and even secretly re-read the story more than once. Job was a good man—upright. Yet God allowed his many possessions to be stripped from him, for his whole family to be crushed by a house in a windstorm, and for his own body to be stricken in pain and covered in boils. After wrestling with God through all that, and after his wife told him to curse God, Job still believed.

I don't think I could ever trust God again. I'm so deeply bitter. So full of *anger*. I still *fume* every time I think about losing Cindy. Then, the salt in the wound, to lose Nate—in a *church* bus crash?

The fallout from my disdain toward God has changed Veronica. She's followed my lead and evolved from an innocent, joyful little girl who had childlike faith, into a blunt, cold, streetwise young woman who doesn't take lip from anybody.

In a way I suppose that's good because life is harsh. She needs to be tough, strong, and able to protect herself.

Of course, that goes against everything we used to believe—blind faith, counting on an ancient, invisible God to protect us, floating along as innocent children thinking nothing bad could ever happen to us.

"How about some hot chocolate, Doug?" Gilbert leans into the room, with an arm against the doorframe.

"No thanks, Gilbert. I'm good."

He disappears back into the kitchen.

It hurt when Veronica called me a zombie and told me to wake up from my slumber.

We would not be in this predicament if Cindy was still alive.

What *am* I going to do about Sebastian and the debt?

Will other people really come here?

Even though I don't really care what happens to me, Veronica is right, I need to protect her and Hale, and Sandra if she's here. I can't move Hale, which means I must be here. Which means I should have a gun.

I overhear Veronica and Gilbert mention Randall Bookman—and suddenly I have the spark of an idea.

I bet Randall has access to guns.

And I also bet he has his portion of that robbery money stashed someplace.

My phone vibrates. I dig it out of my back pocket.

It's a text—from Sebastian: "Can you talk?"

Instantly nervous, I stand up and text back: "Yes."

In a few seconds, my phone rings, and my heart races.

"Yes?" I answer.

"Do you have the money?" Sebastian says.

"No, I told you—"

"Are you going to have it in another . . . twenty-nine hours?"

"Most likely not."

Sebastian heaves a sigh. "I told you before, I like you, Frodele. The situation with your son—it's hard. I get it. But . . . I've just left a meeting with the powers that be."

Long pause.

Now Hale is staring up at me, his brown eyes locked on mine. He's abandoned trying to keep track of Gilbert and has zeroed in on my conversation. *He knows something is wrong.*

"These people are going to do something so horrific that it will *force you* to get the money. Do you understand me? I don't know what they're planning, but from what I know, they are *ruthless*. You've still got twenty-nine hours. Get the money, Douglas, before it's too late. Do it now, for the good of your family."

I just can't believe this is real.

"What will they do?" I say flatly.

"Remove a body part? Kill your son? Hurt Sandra or your daughter? I have no idea. But you have twenty grand of their money, and they will not relent until they have it all back, plus the ten interest."

"Please, isn't there anything you can do?"

"I've done it already! They're livid with me. I've held them off for three weeks."

"One more week—"

"No! It's not up to me. The decision's been made. They're coming tomorrow night with a vengeance. I've told Sandra not to be there and you'd be wise to keep your daughter away. But don't you try to run. They'll find you. Get a loan, man!"

"Can you come here then? Protect us? Make the damage minimal?"

"Oh my gosh, you really do live in a fantasy world. If I showed up there, they'd put a bullet in *my* head. Do you understand? I'm nothing to them but a foot soldier. I have no more pull with them. This is out of my hands now—that's why I'm calling you."

Long pause.

"I'm sorry for you. Good luck." Sebastian ends the call.

Hale blinks at me and a tear shoots down the left side of his face.

13

HALE

It's nothing new for me to turn things over to God.

What options do I have? *LOL*

Although my faith has been tested to the breaking point, overall, it has become stronger since the bus crash. Because, when trouble hits, I have no other recourse than to leave it in his hands—dump it in his lap and forget about it. *What else can I do?* I can't attempt to solve the problem with my own ingenuity, money, intervention, or strength.

Things usually work out pretty well that way.

So that's what I'm forced to do now.

Dad is obviously in a fix. When he wiped the tears from my face and bent over to kiss my forehead, I saw tears in his own eyes.

He's gone now. I saw his car leave about ten minutes after he left my room. I asked God to go with him, to protect him, and to diffuse this timebomb that is ticking toward tomorrow night.

It's out of my hands.

Right now, I can't get any attention from anybody. Gilbert and Veronica are sitting next to each other in my room sipping hot cocoa and gabbing like two town gossips.

Actually, that makes my heart glad. It's good for Veronica to be hitting it off so well with Gilbert—he's a good influence.

Listen to me, I sound like a grandparent.

"I'm surprised I haven't seen you on campus," Veronica says. "I usually hang out at the student union between classes. You ever go there?"

"Eh, rarely," Gilbert says. "I got lucky this semester—all my classes are back-to-back. So I usually get to campus, hit all of them, and head home or to work. I work a lot."

He explains how Fred and Sue are making Ellie and him pay for their own college tuition. And Veronica shares how Dad and Mom had planned on paying for ours—but time and circumstances changed all that.

Gilbert gets up from his chair and comes over to the bed; his limp is barely noticeable. "Hey, buddy," he says. "You didn't expect to see me again so soon, did you?"

He turns to Veronica. "Where's his hat, do you know? I gave it to him. It was on him when I was here earlier."

Cruella took it!

Veronica chuckles. "No. Why did you give him your hat?"

Gilbert makes a funny face. "Did you see his haircut? Jasmine got carried away and I thought he looked cold. It feels like a meat locker in here."

"Tell me about it. Why do you think I'm wearing like five layers?" Veronica stands and points to Gilbert's mug. "You want more?"

"No thanks. I've had enough."

"I'm getting a refill." She heads toward the kitchen. "What're you doing here anyway? You came today, right?"

Gilbert nods, takes a deep breath, and sighs. "Yeah, I just need to talk to him for a few minutes."

Veronica stops and stares at Gilbert.

"You are a really good person, you know that?" she finally says.

"So are you."

She throws her head back and laughs. "I am not. You know I'm not."

"I know who you really are, deep down," Gilbert says. "You just put on a tough exterior."

Veronica stands there and looks at him with glazed eyes and shakes her head. "It's not just an exterior. I've changed Gilbert. Not for the better. I know that."

He stands up and walks over to her. "It doesn't have to stay that way."

Suddenly, her bottom lip quivers and her brown eyes fill with tears. "I'll let you two talk." She leaves abruptly for the kitchen, but calls out, "Text me if you want to talk more later. I'll be in my room."

Hit a nerve with her—that's progress.

Finally, we can get down to business.

Gilbert gets the white stool, sets it by my bed, and sits. He rubs my head.

"We're going to have to find that hat, aren't we?" he says quietly. He stares at me, right in the eyes, for like a minute. "So, bro." He leans closer and lowers his voice. "I need to talk to somebody and I figure who better than my best friend?"

I flinch as my senses kick into high-alert mode.

"I've been doing a lot of thinking and praying the past few days," he whispers, "and you and your family keep coming to my mind. I mean . . . I can't shake it."

With that, I lose it. My whole body locks up.

"Sorry, sorry, sorry." He puts his hands on my rigid shoulders to try to calm me. But I remain buckled up like a stone wall.

"I'm praying for you to get healed. I'm praying for your dad and Veronica to come back to God. And I keep getting this feeling . . . it's like a premonition."

Yes! You're right. You're right!

"Be calm, buddy, be calm. It's okay. Do you know what's going on? Is that it? Is there something going on around here? Is everyone treating you okay?"

I can only grunt and strain and moan, wishing I could scream out about how Sandra treats me—and threatens me.

"What are *you* doing here?"

It's Sandra.

She's entered my room holding yet another glass of who knows what. "These aren't your normal calling hours."

Gilbert looks over at her. "Yeah, no, I just came by . . . I forgot to tell him something earlier."

"Ahh." Sandra tilts her head back in sarcasm. "What was that about a 'premonition?' Are you reading palms now or was that some sort of 'biblical prophecy?'" She chuckles.

Gilbert points at the pocket of her winter vest. "Is that my hat?"

She looks down where he's pointing and, while doing so, loses her balance and spills her drink slightly. She curses, licks the remnants from her glass, and yanks the gray hat from her pocket. "Is that yours?" she tosses it to him. "I wondered whose it was. It didn't look like one of ours."

Gilbert examines the hat and turns back to me. "Good seeing you, Sandra."

"Oh! Is that my cue to leave? To leave my own house?" Her head wags as she says it. "You need to learn some manners, Gilbert."

Gilbert swivels back around toward her. "What *is* going on around here, Sandra? I do have a premonition. Something's not right."

Man, the guy has guts.

She takes a swig and levels her gaze at him. "Sounds like you've been drinking too much of the Christian Kool-Aid, Gilbert."

"At least it's just Kool-Aid." He nods at her drink.

"Oh, well you're just better than everyone else, aren't you—because you don't drink alcohol. And you don't swear or lie or cheat or steal. You're just so good and squeaky clean." She cackles. "Is that why you work at Squeaky's car wash?"

Gilbert shakes his head and is probably thinking, why do I even bother trying to talk to her.

You're such a wench, Sandra! How dare you treat my best friend like that!

"I just want to be alone with Hale for a couple minutes and I'll be out of here." Gilbert turns his back on Sandra and makes a funny face at me.

Sandra swirls her glass in a circular motion, takes a sip, and levels her gaze at Gilbert. "You're not so holy, Gilbert, you know that?"

Gilbert rolls his eyes and turns back around to face her while still sitting on the stool.

"You remember what you called me earlier today?" Sandra says. "Dark, bitter . . . you said my life is *meaningless*. Is that what Jesus would do? I thought you Christians were supposed to love everybody—even your enemies."

Gilbert's head drops.

He's too kind for Sandra's type. He's going to apologize; I can feel it coming.

Gilbert looks up at her. "I've known Hale all my life. He's my best friend. The things you said about him today were cruel. I'm not going to—"

"It's called *reality*, Gilbert." Sandra moves toward him like a snake, jabbing her drink and a finger at him. "These are the cards he's been dealt . . . I've been dealt! It is what it is. You Christians just don't want to face the music. You said earlier I bury this family in unbelief. That's not true. I'm simply a *realist*." She points at me. "He. Is. Brain. Dead. When are you going to get that through your head? I think you come here for yourself. This is like therapy for you."

"He understands what you're saying right now, as sure as I'm sitting here," says Gilbert.

"Pfft. You live in a fairy tale." Sandra walks toward the door. "I guess we're just going to have to agree to disagree."

"Whatever," Gilbert mumbles.

On her way into the kitchen Sandra trips on the floor molding, but doesn't fall, and Gilbert makes a crazy funny face at me. I laugh, which comes out as a deep groan.

Gilbert sighs and shakes his head. He arises from the stool, puts the hat back on my head, and sits back down.

"Let's pray, bro. I've got to get going."

My eyes are locked on him.

He leans his arms on the bed rail. "God, whatever's going on in this house, whatever evil may be happening, whatever unbelief, we pray you'll squelch it. Drive it out. Heal this dude, Lord." Gilbert covers my hands with his. "Touch him. Restore him. Resurrect him. We both know you can do it. Please. Hale needs a miracle . . . We pray, too, for Veronica and Doug. Be real to them again. Drive them back to you."

I hear a buzz, a phone vibrating.

Gilbert digs his phone out of his pocket and examines the screen.

"That's a text from your sister." He begins texting her back. "She needs to tell me something before I leave."

14

DOUGLAS

It's a frigid night and my car crunches to a stop in the remnants of frozen snow that's been plowed to the curb in front of Randall Bookman's house on Bancroft Road in Akron. I turn out the lights and sit here with the heat cranked. I've got twenty-four hours and I don't have any other alternatives.

I turn the car off and walk the wet street to the driveway, being careful not to slip on black ice. There are a million stars in the clear sky tonight. I head up the driveway toward the yellow split-level house. It's a typical blue-collar, Akron home. Back in the day, virtually everyone around here worked at one of the big rubber companies, like Goodrich, Firestone, or Goodyear; but the industry here in The Rubber City Capital of the World has been on the decline since the 1980s.

I walk carefully up the narrow sidewalk that someone has shoveled leading to the front door and wonder if it was Randall who shoveled it. I've never met his parents and I have no idea if he has siblings. They have one of those video doorbells. I ring it and hear it chime inside.

"Victor," a female voice yells from inside. "Someone's at the door. Victor!"

After what seems like a minute the wood door pries open five inches. There's another glass door between me and the short old man who peers out at me. He says nothing.

"Hi. I'm Douglas Frodele. I'm here to see Randall. Is he home?" *He should be home if he's wearing an ankle monitor.*

"What's it about?" the man calls.

"It's about my daughter, Veronica. Randall used to date her."

The door opens a bit more and the slight old man, who has a full head of gray hair and a gray beard, pushes the glass door open.

I start to open the glass door more to go in, but he holds it firmly.

"Are you accusing him of doing something—to your daughter?"

"No, no, no," I say with a chuckle. "It's nothing like that. He's in no trouble with me. I just need to speak to him for a few minutes. Really, it's all fine."

Two minutes later I'm sitting on a couch with bad springs in a warm, cluttered living room. The smell of sauerkraut permeates the place, almost so badly that I want to cover my nose. Stacks of books and magazines are everywhere, along with large skeins of yarn in all colors, and what appear to be bag after bag of sewing projects.

The father has disappeared and I notice the mother looking in at me from what I assume is the kitchen. I start to say hello, but all I see is the whisp of her apron swirling in the doorway and she's gone.

I hear heavy footsteps on the split-level stairs, coming up from the lower level.

Randall appears and stations himself near the top of the steps. "Mr. Frodele?" He's wearing Army green joggers and a white Puma hoodie. His dark brown hair is long, held back by a silk Harley Davidson headband, and he's clean shaven, with sharp facial features. The bulky black ankle monitor is in plain sight above his right foot. He wears camo slippers.

"Randall, hi." I stand. "I'm sorry to show up unannounced."

He stuffs his hands in the front pockets of the hoodie and makes no movement toward me. "What's this about?" He sways back and forth.

"Veronica tells me she saw you at the mall recently."

He nods. "Is that what this is about?"

"Actually, no. I'm here for two reasons." I look around, wondering if the parents could be within earshot. "Are we private here?"

He shrugs, says, "Follow me," and bops down the steps like a rubber ball.

I follow him down to what appears to be his part of the house. It's dark and smells slightly damp. There's a large unmade waterbed, piles of clothes on the floor, and a huge TV screen on the wall that is paused in the middle of a motocross video game. At the far end of the room, there's another room that is unfinished. It has concrete walls and a lone fluorescent light shines down on a table with a motorcycle on it that is half disassembled. Several pictures of motorcycles and race cars are pinned to the walls of the room we stand in, and an old brown metal dehumidifier chugs away in the corner.

"So, what are you doing now?" I say.

He shrugs. "Working at Auto Care Showcase, in the mall."

That makes sense, because GPS monitors can usually only be worn to work and home, or whatever parameters the authorities plug in.

Enough of the small talk.

"Listen, I know about the robbery . . ."

He throws a hand up and shakes his head at me as if to say, "And?"

"I want to propose something to you," I say, my heart beating faster. "If you give me thirty grand of your take of the money, I'll pay it back to you at twenty percent interest."

Randall's head cranes backward with a questioning look on his face. "What are you—wired or something?"

"No, no, no." I step closer to him and hold my coat open. He backs up several steps. "I had to borrow money for things for Hale—medical bills and equipment. I'm in a bind. But, if I can get the money, make this payment, I'll be good. And I'll start saving up your interest. This way, you can be making money while . . . if you have to do any time."

"Whoa! I've not been proven guilty of anything. What the heck, man?"

"Your motorcycle was captured on video, with you on it."

"They don't know that was me. That's a common bike."

"Okay, well, I'm offering you a six-grand return on your money, and you don't have to do a thing for it. You'll be growing your money exponentially while sitting in prison."

"If I *would* get convicted, which I'm not counting on, I may consider it then. But it would take a lot more than six grand for me to make that loan—"

"Nope." I cross my arms and shake my head. "Sorry. This is a one-time offer. I need the thirty now. I'll up the interest from six to seven grand."

Randall sighs and shrugs and shifts his feet. "What's the second thing?"

I stare at him for a few seconds, not even believing I am here doing this.

"I need a gun," I finally say. "Maybe two, depending how much you might charge me."

He squints at me with a painful scowl. "What? What would *you* need a gun for?"

I sigh. "It's all about the money I owe. If I don't pay by tomorrow night I'm going to be in big trouble. They will probably come to the house."

"What about Veronica?"

I nod. "Yeah, right. That's why I need protection."

"Do you even know how to handle a gun?"

"I figured you could show me . . . you know, just show me now, the basics. We don't have to actually shoot it."

Randall's dark eyes narrow at me. "You have a lot of nerve, coming into my house, presuming I'm guilty in that heist, presuming I have guns."

"You're right." I stammer. "I'm just being straight with you because I'm desperate. I can't think of anywhere else to turn. The clock is ticking."

"Number one, you can buy a gun at a gun shop. Number two, you can get a loan from a bank. I'm in enough trouble here." He cusses for emphasis.

I explain that no banks will loan me anymore money, and that because I may be using the gun for illicit purposes, I thought I should get one under the radar.

Randall huffs, shakes his head, and crosses to an old desk that's piled high with junk—ten-pound weights, empty soda and energy drink cans, a matte gray motorcycle helmet, black leather gloves, and a skyline of motocross trophies of all shapes and sizes.

He kneels down and opens one drawer after another; each is filled to the brim with papers, folders, and junk. He finds a small silver vape pipe, turns it on and takes a hit, then exhales a cloud of smoke while continuing his search.

Digging deep in the bottom drawer he finally pulls out a small black revolver with a wood handle. Without a word, he opens the cylinder, dials it, locks it back in, and continues searching the drawers.

That little pea shooter is not exactly what I had in mind, but I guess it may have to do.

Randall eventually collects a handful of bullets and gets to his feet with a grunt.

"You can take this. It's clean. I don't want anything for it." He holds the gun and fistful of bullets out to me. His hands and fingernails are soiled, probably from his work on the motorcycle.

"Thank you." I take the bullets—there are five. "I can pay you for it."

"No. Here. You push this release latch and the cylinder pops open, like this. Load the bullets in." He does it and pushes the bullets in one at a time. "Snap it shut. To fire, you pull this hammer back and pull the trigger. It will keep firing until you go through all the bullets. It holds six but I only found five."

He hands me the gun and it's twice as heavy as it looks. I bounce it in my hand.

"Careful!" he says. "Here." He snatches it from me, snaps the cylinder open, dumps the bullets into his hand, and drops them into my coat pocket. "That's a Colt .38 special, which means it takes thirty-eight caliber bullets if you need to buy more."

"Thank you again, Randall. I hope I didn't—"

"You should go." He walks to the steps.

For some odd reason, I don't want this to end yet. I feel sorry for the kid. And I feel safe with him. I walk toward the steps where he shifts his weight from one foot to the other.

"I'd come to your house tomorrow night myself, if I could." He waves a hand at the ankle monitor. "But I can't."

I nod, genuinely grateful to him. "I'm sorry to have assumed your guilt. I apologize."

"It's all good," he says. "Tell Veronica hey . . . Oh . . . I suppose you won't tell her you came."

I shrug and say I'm not sure, thank him, say goodbye, and head up the stairs.

When I'm near the top, Randall calls my name.

I stop and turn around.

"If you're going to get that thing out in a confrontation—be prepared to use it."

15

HALE

"Sorry about earlier." Veronica walks into my room from the kitchen holding two steaming cups; she hands one to Gilbert. "I haven't gotten emotional like that since Nate's funeral."

"Sometimes it's good to get emotional," Gilbert says. "Thanks for this."

"Careful. Hot-hot."

"What did you want to talk about?" he says.

I feel like I'm eavesdropping, but I'm sitting right here in plain sight.

"Can we sit?" Veronica sits back down where they were earlier, and Gilbert pulls the other chair close to hers and sits.

I love seeing these two chatting again like old friends! Who knows what this might lead to!

"My dad's in trouble," she says.

She proceeds to tell Gilbert about Sebastian's recent visits and the thirty grand Dad owes by tomorrow night. Gilbert asks a bunch of logical questions, like why Dad doesn't get a loan from a bank, and Veronica answers as best she can.

"Who is this Sebastian guy and how'd your dad get involved with him?" Gilbert says.

Veronica chuckles sarcastically. "He's Sandra's friend. They knew each other back in the day. You can't make this stuff up."

"That figures. How dangerous is he? Do you know his last name?"

I hear a car coming up the driveway. It's Dad.

This'll be interesting.

"No idea," Veronica says.

"We should search him anyway. That's an unusual name." Gilbert stands. "You have your laptop?"

"It's in my room." Veronica stands. "I can grab it."

"It'll be easier than doing it on our phones."

"Be right back." Veronica goes into the house.

Gilbert comes over to my bed. "Your sister and I are talking again. What do you think of that?"

My body flinches.

"I know, it's cool, right?" He leans on the rail of my bed. "I knew something was going on. Sounds like your dad may need to get the police involved."

Dad is in the house now. I hear him and Veronica exchange words in the kitchen.

Veronica comes back into my room holding up a silver laptop. "Sandra's was in the kitchen. We can use it."

"Cool."

She hands the computer to Gilbert, they sit back down, and he opens the machine.

A phone vibrates.

Veronica gets out her phone and examines the glowing screen. Her eyes race across the rows of a text message

"What?" she whispers.

"What is it?" Gilbert says.

She looks up at him. "My dad was just at Randall Bookman's house."

"Randall Bookman? What for?"

Veronica shakes her head and stares off. She clenches her teeth. "I'm telling you—he's coming unglued. This is all so . . . messed up!" She crosses her arms, and rocks back and forth.

"Why did he go there?" Gilbert sets the laptop on the small table next to him and leans over his knees, closer to her.

Tears streak down Veronica's face.

"Why did God let mom die?" She stops rocking and stares at Gilbert. "Can you answer that?"

Gilbert sighs and drops back in his chair.

"And why Nate? And why this?" Veronica throws a hand toward me.

Gilbert squints and shakes his head. "I don't know, Veronica. I wonder that all the time. I just don't know."

She sobs. "The life we had, it was . . . a dream. It was like another life."

"I remember."

"Do you? Do you, really?"

Gilbert nods, emphatically.

"What?" she says. "What do you remember?"

He chuckles softly. "Your dad giving us wheelbarrow rides."

Veronica's head drops and she cries.

"Remember? He would dump us in the leaves at the end, over by the burning pile. Your mom would be yelling, 'Careful Douglas. Careful!'"

Veronica nods while her head is still down, and her shoulders bounce from the mixture of laughter and tears.

"Remember how big we would get those leaf piles?" Gilbert says. "They were like ten feet tall. Hale would use that backpack blower that was twice his size."

They both giggle.

Oh, man, do I remember that.

"And your mom and dad would cook breakfast down by the creek," Gilbert continues. "And we would wade in the water and catch crawdads and put them in jars. I loved that. And your mom would lead us on nature walks, remember those?"

Veronica mumbles something and abruptly goes over to the sink, snatches several tissues, comes back, and sits.

"She explained to us which trees were which. She showed us the leaves. I've always known my trees because of your mom," Gilbert says. "She told us all about the different butterflies and insects."

Veronica sniffs and wipes her nose with the tissue. "Remember that time my dad came with us and tied us all together with that rope? We looked like we were going to climb Mount Everest."

"And we each had our own big walking stick!"

They both lean back and roar.

"I think that's the time we got lost," Gilbert says.

I'm laughing, too, because I remember it all as if it was yesterday.

"Sounds like I'm missing out on all the fun." Dad enters the room, rubbing his hands together. "It's nice to hear laughter around here."

Veronica dabs her eyes with a tissue and her face instantly becomes sober. She stands and sticks a hand on her hip and looks at Dad. "You went to Randall's house? Are you for real?"

My sister's never been one to mince words.

Dad deflates, glances at Gilbert, and looks back at Veronica. "It was just an idea."

"It was more than an idea, apparently. Let's see it." She holds her hand out toward Dad, palm up.

He squints at her, shakes his head, and flicks his eyes toward Gilbert and back to her. "Let's wait and talk about this alone, okay?" Dad says.

"I've already told Gilbert about Sebastian and the money you owe," Veronica says.

Dad heaves a sigh and looks out into the night, and Veronica addresses Gilbert. "He tried to borrow money from Randall at a high rate of interest. And he got a gun from him. Let's see it, Dad."

Gilbert stands and we all wait for Dad to say something.

He holds his empty hands up. "It's a simple revolver. There's nothing to see. It's just in case of trouble tomorrow night."

"Why don't you call the police?" Gilbert says.

"Oh, nooooo," Veronica says sarcastically. "That would be too practical. Doug can handle it on his own."

"Sebastian's a loan shark," Dad barks. "It's illegal."

"So, you tell the police that," Veronica says. "Better for you to get in a little trouble with the law than in a lot of trouble with some—loan shark."

"It's not that simple," Dad says. "If I get the police involved, Sebastian, or whoever he works for . . . well, they won't be happy."

"You mean they'll hurt you," Veronica clarifies, bluntly.

"Yes," Dad says. "Maybe. Probably."

"Pick your poison," Veronica says.

"Doug, you've got to call the police," Gilbert insists.

"What do you know about it, Gilbert?" Sandra enters the room loud and proud.

Gilbert looks at her but says nothing.

"So, now *he* knows our dirty laundry," Sandra says, pointing at Gilbert.

"So, what?" Veronica says. "What difference does it make if he knows? He's been part of this family longer than you have."

"Please!" Dad shouts and raises a stiff hand. "It's bad enough without more turmoil. Just, can we not argue?"

"Pfft. You're pathetic." Sandra heads for the door, then stops and turns back around to face us all. "You realize why we're in this mess, right?" She raises an arm and points toward me. "It's him! You refuse to face the facts about that."

"Stop!" Veronica yells. "Shut up, Sandra! Just go . . . have another drink. Watch your stupid shows. Just get out. You know nothing about this family."

"Are you going to stand there and let her talk to me like that?" Sandra yells at Dad.

He turns his back on all of us.

Sandra stands there, shellshocked. She looks at Gilbert, then Dad, then Veronica; she doesn't even bother to glance my way.

"To hell with all of you." She disappears into the house.

16

HALE

It's early Wednesday morning and getting light outside. There is even a bit of golden sunshine casting long, stark morning shadows on the snow from the many trees in the back woods. The rich smell of coffee drifts into my room from the kitchen.

Tonight is the night.

Dad is hurrying around, eating a bowl of cereal, checking his phone, and starting my morning feeding. He's wearing his U.S. postal carrier uniform—the light blue shirt and gray pants with the dark stripe down the side, and the black waterproof boots.

His mind is somewhere else as he connects the g-tube to my port with his cold hands, flushes it with water, hooks up the food pouch, hangs it on the IV pole, and turns on the food pump. He's probably thinking about tonight's showdown with Sebastian, or whoever may show up here for the money Dad doesn't have. I watch as the clay-colored liquid food slowly curls its way down the clear tube into my stomach.

What I wouldn't give for a bacon-egg-and-cheese biscuit.

After Sandra bowed out last night, the rest of us mulled around in silence for a few more minutes. Gilbert offered to come over tonight to be with me while Dad deals with Sebastian, but Dad insisted he not come. *I wouldn't put it past Gilbert to show up anyway.*

Sandra is nowhere to be found because she usually sleeps in like a teenager.

I AM IN HERE

I hear a low hum outside and see a humongous, unfamiliar dark burgundy SUV rolling up the driveway with steam billowing out its twin exhaust system.

Dad doesn't hear it and throws on his navy winter uniform jacket with the red and white horizontal stripe across the chest and sleeves. He comes over and checks the pouch of food hanging on the IV rack next to my bed.

"I hope you have a good day, buddy." He notices Gilbert's ski cap on my pillow and works it back onto my head. "If you think of it today, pray about this money we owe. I'd be lying if I told you I'm not nervous."

The doorbell rings.

Dad checks his watch and mumbles 'who can that be' as he grabs his navy fur uniform cap with the floppy ears and leaves the room.

I hope the bad guys haven't arrived early.

There's muffled talk in the distant foyer and I'm straining to hear. It's another male. Whoever it is, they'll come in here. Dad always ends up bringing visitors in here.

Dad offers coffee but the man doesn't want any.

As predicted, they spill into my room from the kitchen.

"You haven't seen Hale since the accident, have you?" Dad says.

Oh, wow. It's our old assistant pastor, Rick Powers. The dude has lost like eighty pounds.

"No, I haven't." He walks right over to my bed and looks down at me with a smile. "Hi, Hale. Do you remember me? I'm Rick."

My body flinches involuntarily.

"He remembers," Dad says. "Excuse me a minute, Rick. Let me call work and have someone start sorting my mail."

"I like that hat," Rick says to me. "Mark has one very similar. Do you remember Mark?"

I hear myself groan.

Of course I remember your son. Pretty good kid. Graphic novel nut. A year younger than me. And you have other kids, too. Mark's the oldest.

"What a great view you have, Hale. I remember this used to be the back porch. You've got a good setup here. I miss seeing you at church."

Rick makes more small talk and actually seems to be genuinely trying to connect with me, which is refreshing.

Dad finishes his call.

"That'll give me a few extra minutes," he says. "What can I do for you, Rick?"

Rick clears his throat. "I haven't been able to stop thinking about you . . . since you came to the church. Didn't sleep much last night."

Dad's head drops.

This is all news to me.

"I'd like to try to help you, Doug."

Dad looks up at him but says nothing.

"I didn't say anything about the video to Pastor Brent after you left. For all he knows, I went ahead and helped you out—from the Benevolence Fund."

He's talking about Pastor Brent Miller from our old church. I don't understand what's transpired between them recently, but I am getting my hopes up.

"Why, Rick?"

"Because—you need help."

"But . . . after what I did."

Rick nods. "It seems like you're pretty desperate."

"I am."

"We can't do thirty thousand. I'm sorry."

"I know it's a lot." Dad frowns and blinks.

"We can do fifteen thousand. Will that help you?"

Dad pauses and I know the wheels are turning in his head.

"That's very generous of you," Dad finally says. "Yes. That will help immensely."

Rick nods, reaches inside his coat, and pulls out a checkbook and pen. Without another word, he scribbles out a check, tears it off, and hands it to Dad.

"Wow." Dad shakes his head. "I don't know what to say."

"It's not from me, Doug. It's from God—and a generous congregation."

Dad examines the check, which he holds in both hands. "Well, I . . . I'm beyond grateful."

Rick heads toward the kitchen. "Will you stay in touch?"

I AM IN HERE

"Absolutely," Dad says, but I doubt it's true; I *know* it's not true.

They head into the house and their voices fade as Dad ushers Rick to the front door.

I hear a cupboard open and coffee being poured, then footsteps.

"Good morning." Sandra's deep, raspy morning voice jolts me. She makes her way over to my bed, clutching her Game of Thrones coffee mug in both hands. "How is our wonder boy this morning?"

I have no idea why she calls me that, other than to infuriate me.

She stands next to my bed with the steaming mug up by her chin, surveying the snow-covered property out my window.

"Finally, some sun." She sounds like she's just smoked a pack of Winston's.

I hear the front door close.

Sandra leans over my bed rail. "Get ready for the Academy Award performance of the year."

What's that supposed to mean?

Dad hurries into my room and stops suddenly when he sees Cruella.

Pastor Rick's car rolls down the driveway and Sandra sees it.

"That was Rick Powers," Dad says. "He gave us half the money —from the church Benevolence Fund."

Sandra sets her mug down and faces Dad.

He comes to the opposite side of my bed, examines the screen on the pump, and waits for the last of my breakfast to enter my stomach.

"We need to talk, Douglas," Sandra says.

After flushing the g-tube with water, Dad disconnects it from my port, gathers the tube, pouch, and pump, and heads for the sink. "What about?"

Sandra turns and stares at him as he washes the equipment.

He continues scrubbing and rinsing with his back to her.

She remains where she is, right by my bed.

Dad finally finishes, grabs a towel, and dries his hands as he walks over to us.

"I want this to work, Douglas," Sandra says. "Let's make up. Let's make this work. I know we can do it. We've been dealt a bad hand, but it's not too late."

Dad zips up his coat, staring at Sandra as if she's speaking a foreign language.

"I want us to be like we were when we first met," she continues. "Do you remember how in love we were?"

Dad shrugs. "What brought this on?"

"We deserve to be happy, Doug. We *were* happy."

"Yeah. Then life happened and here we are."

She nods. "And we've both been bitter. With good reason. But that can change. It's already changing. Look, you have half the money now. See? We're meant to break out of this."

"We're still fifteen grand short."

"I can take on more work or find a better job. We can stall them some more. I can try to talk to Sebastian, get us more time."

Dad shakes his head. "What's changed—since last night? Why are you doing this?"

Sandra goes to him. She looks into his eyes and puts her hands on his shoulders. She's wearing those stiff dark blue jeans and those hideous cowboy boots.

"I see what I have and I don't want to lose it," she says as softly as she can. "We can still make it; I know we can."

She whips around and throws a hand toward me.

"I can do better with Hale . . . and Veronica."

These are lies.

She turns back to Dad, reaches up, and touches his cheek. "Please, Doug, give me a chance. Can we start over?"

Don't fall for it, Dad!

Dad reaches up and grasps her wrist. "I want it to work, too."

She mashes her face against his hand that holds her wrist. "We need to focus on each other again, like we did when we first met."

Dad pulls away slightly and stares at her. "We've got to make it through tonight."

She nods and kisses his hand. "We will. We will. We'll find a way. Just wait and see."

17

HALE

A loud noise from the kitchen, the dishwasher door slamming, wakes me up. Sandra is notorious for fighting with the dishwasher; she curses and blabs something I can't understand. I must've fallen back to sleep after Dad left for work.

It's mid- to late-morning and I remember Jasmine isn't coming today.

Naturally, Sandra's got my TV on one of the shopping channels and won't think twice about me today.

I wonder if Veronica left for classes while I was snoozing.

Now I hear the recorded voice of a female doctor. She's talking in a somber tone about a 57-year-old male cancer patient. She describes his dismal diagnosis and her treatment plan. It's an audio recording by one of Sandra's clients. She plays the physicians' recordings and transcribes them. Her fingers clack away at the keyboard on her laptop in the kitchen.

The product being advertised on the massive screen in front of me is a Bluetooth speaker that also serves as a phone charger, clock, and mood lamp with eight different colors.

And today only, of course, it's just $19.95, with free shipping.

The sun is in and out, which is refreshing. We don't see much of it during winter here in the Rust Belt.

While dad is working his route today, I suppose he'll stop at the bank at some point to get the fifteen thousand in cash.

My stomach churns anxiously as I anticipate the night ahead and think back on Sandra's words about her Academy Award performance. What was all that sweet talk about making it work with Dad, and doing better with me and Veronica?

I don't believe any of it.

The tea kettle in the kitchen whistles and Sandra's audio recording stops. Time for Cruella's late-morning tea. It's the same routine almost every day. She tracks down her Game of Thrones mug—if Veronica hasn't hijacked it—and pours hot water over, count them, *three* Zen teabags.

"Sebastian, hey, it's Sandra Frodele. It's 10:50 Tuesday morning. Call me back ASAP when you get this. It's about tonight. Thanks."

Hmm. Maybe she really is going to try to get more time out of Sebastian.

No matter what her motives are, that's what we need—more time.

But how much control over it does Sebastian really have?

The doctor's audio recording comes on again in the kitchen.

Then it goes off.

"Hey," Sandra answers her phone.

"It's about tonight," she says. "Doug's come up with fifteen grand."

I assume it's Sebastian returning her call. I can't hear what he's saying and wish she'd put him on speaker.

"I know, I know," she says, "but half is worth *something*, right?"

Pause.

"Okay, okay, so I've been thinking about this. You just said there's going to be some sort of retaliation for not having all the money, so let me propose something to you," Sandra says.

Pause.

"What if you, or one of your guys, were to show up tonight, get the fifteen grand, and poison the boy, Hale."

I flinch so hard that my bed jolts.

"This would be like your retaliation for us not having all the money, get me? It would be your harsh warning to Doug to come up with the rest of the money."

Long pause.

"Well, I would do it. I've researched it. But it would look like you and your people did it," Sandra explains.

My eyes bulge and feel like they're popping out of their sockets.

"Why would I suggest such a thing? Because—the kid is the reason we're in this mess. He's cost us into the six figures, easily. He's ruined my marriage. And you guys need blood to be spilled. It's a win-win. He can be the sacrificial lamb."

The blood drains from my face.

I'm suddenly nauseous.

"It's clean and simple. I just add a little something to his normal feeding . . . sodium, vodka, hand sanitizer—I haven't decided yet."

My face is on fire and I'm frozen.

I force myself to breathe.

"His brain swells up or he has a seizure. I mean, it *could* look like an accident. I've come close to doing it a hundred times. But you guys don't want it to look like an accident, of course."

My head feels like it's going to explode. White stars are spinning by like I'm on a merry-go-round.

"Since we have half the money, maybe you can come alone tonight. That would make the whole thing easier. You can distract Doug while I do the dirty deed."

Pause.

"Come on, Sebastian, you're a good salesman. I bet you can convince them."

Pause.

"Okay, that's all I can ask. Let me know as soon as you know . . . okay. Bye."

Sandra is putting her phone in her back pocket as she re-enters my room.

"My, my, my—what's wrong with you?"

She comes over to my bed and stares at me with a questioning glare. "Relax, Hale." She looks genuinely shocked at my appearance. "You look like you just saw a zombie." She reaches for me with both hands. I try to recoil, but instead remain ramrod stiff and trembling violently.

"My gosh, lay back. You didn't hear that conversation, did you?"

I hear something, someone in the kitchen.

Veronica enters my room with an alarmed look on her face.

"What did you do to him?" Veronica rushes over to me, barging in front of Cruella.

Thank God!

"I didn't do anything... I just found him like this."

"Hale. Hale!" Veronica grabs my wrists and gets right up in my face. "Settle down. Relax! You're okay. Calm down! You're fine. Okay? Breathe. Just breathe."

I'm doing it... I'm doing what she says.

I'm easing up.

"That's it," Veronica says with a trembling voice.

I'm tentatively settling back down, like a slowly deflating balloon.

My head drops to the pillow and sweat trickles from my forehead down my face. Veronica wipes my face with the rag, adjusts the hat on my head, and turns to Sandra. "What the heck happened?"

"Don't you raise your voice to me. I have no idea."

"Something obviously happened!" Veronica says.

Cruella turns her back and stalks toward the kitchen. "How am I supposed to know. I'm not a nurse."

Veronica turns back to me, and I cry out to her with my eyes, searching her face. She covers my crippled hands in hers. "It's okay, bud. Everything is okay. I'm not going to let anything happen to you."

Her eyes flick up to look outside and a tear streaks down her face. She stares at the winter landscape and slowly shakes her head.

I feel her pain.

We lost mom.

We lost Nate.

We lost our whole beautiful way of life.

Dad's different now.

And we've got a stranger living in our house who is the exact opposite of our real mom.

"Don't you have somewhere to be?" Sandra calls from the kitchen. "He's fine. I'll keep an eye on him."

Veronica looks at her watch. Her head drops. She sniffs and

wipes her nose with the back of her wrist. "I've got a class, bud," she says softly. "Just one today. I've got to get ready. I'll be back soon."

She stands and I look at her.

She leans over my bed. "Don't you worry. I'll take care of Cruella."

I flinch from an eruption of emotion.

Veronica pats my head and breezes into the kitchen.

I listen for an exchange between she and Sandra but hear nothing.

After a few moments, footsteps come toward me.

Sandra again.

She leans against the doorframe leading into my room. "You're finished, 'bud,'" she whispers, mimicking Veronica. "You've taken up too much *space* and too much *money* and too much *attention* for *too long*. It ends tonight. Now, if you are in there by chance, and you understand what I'm saying, and you're worth keeping alive, tell me not to do it, right now . . . Come on, say it, or shake your head, or raise your hand . . ."

My mind sears white and my ears ring.

I am drowning in a black sea of fear and hatred.

I can't do any of those things!

I'm trying but I can't move a muscle.

I don't think I'm breathing.

Somewhere deep in my soul, Gilbert's words alight: "Only believe."

Nothing else.

Sandra smacks her hand on the doorframe. "Precisely what I thought. Not a peep." And she disappears into the kitchen.

18

DOUGLAS

The bank almost didn't give me the fifteen grand. Apparently, a slew of red flags go up when you try to withdraw anything over ten thousand. At first, they told me it would take several days. But I pleaded with them to call Pastor Rick, which they finally did. The ordeal took thirty-five minutes, but the money is now sitting in a U.S. Mail bag next to me on the floor of my postal truck.

Due to the delay at the bank, my route has run later than usual. I'm on Meridian Drive in Fairlawn now, large homes on substantial lots with towering trees—and the last street on my route. It's about 3:55 p.m. and even though it's still cold, the sun has been out much of the day, melting some of the snow and leaving the roads glistening and streaming with runoff.

All day I've reflected on what Sandra said this morning, about not wanting to lose what we had, trying to make it work, and doing better with Veronica and Hale. She hasn't shown that kind of humility in a long time. Honestly, I've felt like it was over for months now. But, if we can just get this awful debt behind us, maybe we can salvage something.

I close the black metal door of the mailbox at the Carter's house, the last on my route, swing the truck around the cul-de-sac, and put it in park, as always. I hop out, trot around back, open the door, get everything organized, and make sure all boxes have been delivered. I jump back in, peek in the bag at the stacks of hundreds, heave a sigh, and head toward the Akron postal office.

This money is going to buy us more time.

As I roll through the puddles, past the large, well-kept estates, I shake my head, thinking how nice it must be to live in one of these homes where money is no object. Oh, sure, some of them are in debt up to their eyeballs, but many are not. Many of these places are paid for, *and* they have second and third homes at the beach or in the mountains.

I had worked my way up to head of client services at the shipping company where I'd spent sixteen years and was making really good money and saving a lot—until Cindy died. Then everything changed. I just couldn't deal with people. A darkness and quiet anger consumed me. It didn't come out in my expression toward others; I suppressed it. But it made me not want to be around anyone. I just went silent, even with the kids.

My bosses at the shipping company gave me plenty of time to snap out of my funk, but I never did. As the weeks went on, they became frustrated with me. Between that and my own realization that I no longer wanted to deal with a gazillion people each day, I left in a fog.

I met Sandra one day at a coffee shop when I was between jobs. In fact, I was literally between interviews when we met. She told me about the opening at the post office. She asked me out. We actually went to a Browns' watch party. We talked and laughed. I hadn't laughed like that since before Cindy was diagnosed. Of course, all of this was when Hale and Nathaniel were healthy and independent—before the church bus wreck that changed everything.

Sandra handled the aftermath of the bus accident well. She pretty much planned the entire memorial service for Nate. And when it came to Hale's recovery, she was all in—for about six weeks. But once we got him home and realized he was likely always going to be in the same vacant state, and require tireless care around the clock, she checked out.

It was as if, one day, she drew a line in the sand. She stepped over that line and left me, Hale, and Veronica on the other side. And we've had nothing but trials and tension ever since.

I can't say I've done much to help matters. I know I'm bitter. And I don't care. When you've been through the trauma and grief I've been through, you just go numb and let it ride. *Who cares?*

There is one thing I've silently been wrestling with and have never mentioned to anyone. When I met Sandra, I had plenty of money in savings and in the stock market. Cindy and I had saved, mainly to pay for college educations, weddings, and retirement. I also received a fair-sized death benefit from Cindy's life insurance policy after she died.

Sandra knew all that.

So, when the accident happened . . . funny, isn't it? We call it an 'accident,' but there are no accidents with God, are there? Nothing slips through his fingers. He knew Cindy and Nate were going to die young. He knew Hale would end up like he is. He *allowed* these tragedies.

How am I supposed to deal with that? Accept that?

Only time will tell if God and I mend.

Right now that's a blank with me.

I just don't bother going there.

Anyway, between Nathaniel's funeral and Hale's months in intensive care at Akron General and weeks at the Neurological Institute at Cleveland Clinic, we spent all the money I'd saved. My insurance covered a lot, but we still owed hundreds of thousands of dollars. Rehab, equipment, food, and nurses continued to drain our accounts.

Bottom line—Sandra thought she was getting into a pretty attractive financial situation when she married me. And now we don't have a penny to our name. Part of my depression stems from the question—did she really ever love me at all?

I was not loveable after Cindy died.

Could Sandra be that cold? That calculated? That desperate?

No. No way.

She loved me.

I've just changed as a result of all the tragedy. I've grown cold and bitter and numb. It's probably all my fault and I've been too self-possessed to see it.

I swing into headquarters and park my truck in the lot with all the others, grab the bag of money, lock the truck, and head for my car. As I get it warmed up, I contemplate calling Sandra to learn if she's been able to reach Sebastian to tell him about the fifteen thousand and get another extension.

Even if that happens, I do not know where I can come up with even one more dime.

I used to pray about such things.

My phone rings over the car speakers as I head out of the parking lot toward home, which is just a short drive. I glance at the caller ID and see it's Pastor Rick calling. I don't want to talk to him but figure it's better to get it out of the way; plus I owe him.

"Hey Rick," I answer.

"Doug, hey. Listen, the bank called me earlier . . ."

Uh oh, I know what he's going to say.

"Yeah, yeah, I know. I asked them to."

"Oh?"

"They weren't going to give me the benevolence money without your approval."

"Yeah, but I was surprised you were getting cash. I assumed you would be writing a check or two—to whoever you owe."

My face flushes because I have no excuse prepared.

"No, no." My mind reels. "I needed the cash to make these payments. It's a long story, but yeah. So, thanks for approving it, Rick. We're good. It's all good."

I hold my breath and he says nothing.

The line just hums as I make the turn onto our long, country road.

Finally, Rick breaks the silence. "Doug, I'm sorry. I shouldn't have approved it without more of an explanation than that. I'm responsible for that money. It's been given by people who want to help those in need—"

"What do you think I'm going to do, Rick, go buy a new car or a hot tub?" I say, angrily. "We're in dire straits here."

I'm a total jerk and I'm just trying to say anything to get him to leave me alone. This is an awful place to be. What kind of a lowlife have I become?

"Just tell me who exactly the money is going to, Doug. That's what I need to know. Are you paying a medical equipment company? Hospital bills? Doctor bills?"

"All that," I blurt.

"But why cash?" Pastor Rick says bluntly. "Just answer me straight out."

I let out a heavy sigh. "You're just going to have to trust me on it, Rick."

"No, Doug! I'm sorry. This is my job and reputation on the line. I need a better answer than that. Where are you right now? I think we need to meet."

19

HALE

Veronica is sitting in a chair next to me still wearing her winter coat with the white fur collar and her beige Ugg boots still wet from the snow. Somehow, she's peeling and eating a cheese stick and, at the same time, scrolling through her phone at a hundred miles an hour. She got home about ten minutes ago from her class, found out Sandra hadn't fed me, and hooked up my dinner pouch, mumbling a few choice words for Cruella as she did.

It's just gotten dark out so I'm guessing it's about 4:30 p.m.

If Sebastian got back to Sandra about tonight, I didn't hear it.

I may have been snoozing.

I don't know if we have more time to pay, or not. I don't know if Sebastian's coming tonight, or his henchmen. It's all up in the air.

Sandra hasn't been in my room since this morning. *No surprise there.*

Veronica laughs at something, expands a photo on her phone, and examines it with her face two inches from the screen.

When I get better, I'm not even going to have a stupid phone. It's insane how much time people waste on them when they could be talking with each other—or going for a walk outside, feeling the sun on their faces, or just enjoying each new day they've been given.

Dad should be home soon.

I'm just trying to do what Gilbert said—*only believe.*

Only believe God will protect me from what Sandra talked about earlier—ending my life tonight . . . only believe God will protect us from Sebastian and his people . . . only believe God will smooth out the problem with the money we owe . . . only believe he'll help Dad and Veronica turn back to him.

Only believe he'll heal me.

We have a car outside, but I can tell from the sound of the engine it's not Dad. It sounds more like . . . I strain to see . . . yep. Pastor Rick Powers again, pulling up in the huge dark burgundy SUV.

What could he want?

He backs the big car in close to dad's shed, puts it in park, and leaves the engine running.

Hmm.

Veronica tips her head back, finishes the last of her cheese stick, stands, and sheds her heavy coat.

Sandra enters my room, crosses to the window, and peers down at Pastor Rick's car. "I wonder what he's doing back?"

Veronica walks over and looks out. "Who is that?"

"A living angel! Pastor Rick Powers. He gave your dad half the money from the church benevolence fund."

"What? That's great," Veronica says. "Will they leave Dad alone now—for a while?"

"Afraid not," Sandra says. "You don't offer these people half of what you owe them—three weeks late. By the way, I reserved a room for you at the Holiday Inn Express in Montrose. You can check in any time now. I may or may not join you. There are two double beds."

"I'm not going anywhere," Veronica fumes.

"Yes, you are. That's one of the few things your father and I agree on. We don't know what's going to happen here tonight. The fewer of us here, the better. In fact, you should throw some things together now and get going. I'll be over later probably."

"I want to see Dad before I go."

"Fine. Get a bag ready now. He should be home soon . . . I wonder why the pastor's sitting in his car? Strange."

Veronica unclips my empty food pouch from the metal hook above me. "So, who's showing up tonight? Do we even know?"

I AM IN HERE

Sandra stares at Veronica while she takes my food equipment to the sink to wash. "Not sure. I hope it's only Sebastian. I haven't heard back from him."

"What time?" Veronica says.

"I have no clue," Sandra says.

"What about dinner?" Veronica says.

"Frozen chicken patties. Everybody's on their own. You can grab one before you go."

"Lovely. Another wholesome family meal."

"Hey, if you don't like it . . . I don't see you making any five course meals around here."

Veronica's frustrated. She misses Mom. Misses the way things used to be. Just like I do. Having Sandra in her place is like a bad dream. That's on Dad. He made the decision to marry her.

Speaking of Dad, I think I hear his car.

Yep. He pulls up the driveway and slows when he sees Pastor Rick's SUV.

He stops his car and sits there.

Pastor Rick's door opens and he unfolds out of the car and stands there between the open door and the car, staring at Dad.

Dad's window goes down and he says something to Pastor Rick.

Pastor Rick throws up his hands and yells something back.

This does not look like an amicable meet up.

20

DOUGLAS

The sun is well down behind the trees as I drive up the driveway, my stomach churning with anxiety over the night ahead.

No.

Pastor Rick's car...

Everything in me goes dark.

I slow down.

I stop.

No, no, no...

His car is backed in, parked, and running. He's in it. A cloud of exhaust streams gently out the back.

I'm gripped by an overwhelming sense of desperation. I glance down at the bag of money on the floor next to me.

He can't take it.

Pastor Rick opens his door, slowly gets out, stands there, and nods at me with a serious face.

I pause then roll down my window. "Hey man. What's up?"

It's so obvious I'm stalling, deceiving . . . if it weren't so serious it would be comical.

Pastor Rick insists we need to talk.

In that split second, I contemplate flying backwards and taking off. *But I can't.* It makes no sense. I can't run from my own home. Plus, I need to be here to make the deal.

I'm still stopped in the middle of the driveway. I yell over to him, "Let me pull in."

After pausing, trying to figure out what to do, I ease the car forward and open the garage door with the remote. I'm light-headed because I have no idea what I'm going to tell Rick. I can't tell him the truth or he'll take the money back. As my car crunches through the snow in the cold dark shade of the house, I decide I will park quickly in the garage and get outside fast—away from the car and money.

As I pull into the garage my phone vibrates.

I park, turn off the car, and look at my phone. A text from Sandra: "What is the pastor doing here?"

Quickly I text back: "He knows I cashed the check. Doesn't like it."

I get out, shut the car door, and hurry outside.

Pastor Rick has trudged toward me up the slight incline and is only fifteen feet from me. He has on a heavy dark blue parka and an army green ski hat.

"Doug, you have to talk to me about getting cash," he says, slightly out of breath. "I need to know everything's on the up and up. Otherwise, the deal's off."

No, no, no.

I chuckle anxiously.

He has every right to doubt me, especially after he saw on video that I was casing out the safe in his office.

He is in the right here; I am in the wrong.

I hold my hand out for him to stop walking, not wanting him to get any closer to the money. "Rick, I promise you every cent of that money is going toward the debts we owe on Hale, just like I told you. Can you just trust me on this? Please?"

Of course, that isn't true because a large chunk of the money is for interest.

He shakes his head and continues toward me. "No, Doug. I can't. What kind of hospital or medical company would require you to pay in cash? Just tell me what's going on. Tell me the truth. Quit messing around with me. I've been good to you here . . . you owe me the truth."

"Would you just stop walking? Stop!" My breath steams into the air and I'm surprised by my own outburst and unsure what I'm going to do.

He stops and leans back, out of breath, and stares at me with a scowl.

I look up. Sandra is staring down at us from Hale's room.

Rick's eyes follow where mine are looking and he sees Sandra, too.

I turn back to Rick. "Can't you just leave this alone, Rick?" I soften my tone. "Please. Just go home."

He shakes his head and puts his hands on his hips. "I need that cash back, Doug. I obviously made a mistake giving it to you. Just give it to me and we'll forget this ever happened. I promise. I'll tell no one."

He begins walking toward me again.

My hands shoot up defensively, as if blocking him from the garage.

I feel like a deranged criminal.

He stops.

Sandra is now gone from the window.

"Look at you, Doug," he says. "You look like a scared animal that's been backed into a corner."

I drop my hands and try to appear normal, but the adrenaline and fear of losing the money has my head buzzing with static.

"What's really going on?" he says. "Is it drugs?"

I'm silent.

Out of nowhere, the garage door lurches to life and begins going down.

Sandra closed it!

Rick clenches his teeth and shakes his head with regret and frustration as the garage door seals shut leaving the cold evening air silent.

"Give me the money now Doug, or I'm calling the police. Straight up."

The word 'police' triggers an internal alarm that reverberates from my head to my toes. "This is the trust you show me?" I plead.

"Shut up, Doug. You think I'm stupid?"

"Of course not—"

"It *was* stupid of me to change my mind and give it to you after seeing that video of you looking for the safe."

"No it wasn't, Rick. You're helping a family in need."

"Stop Doug! No more lies. Take me inside. Give me the money."

I shake my head. "That can't happen, man. I need that money."

"Then I've got to call the police. I don't want to do that. I don't have time for this, Doug."

I hold my hands up and shake my head.

Rick turns on a dime, starts walking toward his car, working his phone out of his coat pocket. It's almost completely dark now. He stops and punches the glowing screen.

He's calling the police!

"Don't, Rick!" I yell, jogging toward him, my mind blind with desperation.

He has the phone to his ear.

I get to him and he squares up to me, holding up a defensive hand.

He's much taller than me.

"This is not an emergency, but I do need some officers to come out to—"

I lunge at him and grab the phone, but he doesn't let go.

We fight frantically for the phone.

"Stop!" Rick growls.

We both seethe and whimper and grunt as we wrestle for the phone.

I can't believe I'm doing this.

He finally rips the phone away and glares at me, frozen and out of breath.

He thinks I'm deranged.

He holds the palm of his hand open and examines it; it's bleeding from our scuffle. He bends down and swooshes it in the snow, which is left red from the blood.

He straightens with a groan and examines his phone.

I assume the call got disconnected, because he drops his hands and holds the phone at his side as he heads the last few steps for his SUV, staggering slightly.

He didn't deserve this. He was just trying to help!

The misery of my sinfulness weighs me down like a led vest.

Rick stops at his car door, looks at his phone, and punches the screen.

Just as I'm about to give up and go inside, resolving that the police will come, I hear a car rumbling up the driveway.

I wait and watch. So does Rick.

Sebastian!

Sandra must've called him.

The red, older model Cadillac looks menacing as it glides in with just its orange parking lights glowing. It slows and almost stops as Sebastian assesses the situation. Then the car roars slightly and rolls surprisingly quickly directly in front of Rick's SUV, only three feet from his front bumper, and stops.

Rick has his phone to his ear and when he sees how the Cadillac has blocked him in, he opens his car door, looking unsure what to do.

Sebastian is out of his car faster than I thought he could move. He's bundled up like a dog sled driver—and he has a large black gun with a silencer pointed directly at Rick.

21

HALE

Ho-ly smokes! Sebastian has a gun stuck in Pastor Rick's gut and he's taking his phone from him!

Dad is standing in the driveway with them, tense as a cat, his hands out as if pleading with Sebastian to calm down and to not hurt Rick.

What's Dad gotten us into?

Sandra called Sebastian in a huff a few minutes ago, urging him to get over here because 'that goody two-shoes pastor' was going to take his cash back.

"Veronica Frodele!" Sandra yells from the kitchen toward the stairs. "Get down here. You need to *go!*"

Sandra breezes into my room and looks out the window down toward the altercation.

"You're watching the whole thing, aren't you?" she says to me. "I can barely see anymore, it's getting so dark."

We could both see better outside if you'd turn the gigantic TV off for once!

"Your sister needs to get the heck out of Dodge," she mutters. "All hell is going to break loose here soon . . . What are they doing down there?"

"What's the big rush?" Veronica appears in the doorway to my room.

Sandra turns to face her and thumbs toward the window. "It's starting and you're still here. Tell me you're packed."

Veronica looks down at the brown overnight bag on the floor next to her and looks up at Sandra.

"Good," Sandra says. "Now get going. I'll be over in a bit."

Veronica sees me all cockeyed, staring out the window into the winter night. She walks to the window and looks out. "What's going on now? Whose car is that?"

"Sebastian's," Sandra says with her hands cupped around her eyes, against the window.

"Is that a gun?" Veronica screams. "My gosh, Sandra, what's going on?"

"Get your coat on and go, *now*. Take the van. Just back it out and go. They'll get out of the way."

"The van? Can't I take Dad's car?"

"Will you just do as I ask?" Sandra barks. "We don't exactly have time right now to discuss your choice of vehicles."

Veronica turns the TV off as well as the lamp next to my bed. She hurries back to the window and looks down on the dark scene. "OMG! They're bringing Pastor Rick up here with a gun in his back. You have got to be kidding me! How stupid can you be!"

I don't like this—but maybe all the commotion will prevent Sandra from hurting me.

Sandra crosses to Veronica and grabs her left arm. "You need to get out of here, now. Go! I'm not asking again."

Veronica rips her arm away. "Get your hands off me. This is my house. Why do you want me gone so bad? Why aren't you coming now? I don't trust you."

Finally, someone with sense!

Sandra's body braces and her eyes widen. "You've been nothing but a thorn in my side since I married your dad." She growls through clenched teeth. "You and your whole generation are a bunch of spoiled brats. Now get out of here before I strangle you!"

With the last words, Sandra reaches for Veronica's throat and Veronica shoves her hand away. Sandra comes at her again and Veronica bashes her hands away, harder this time.

Veronica's no wimp.

Everything in me wants to bolt up and defend her.

I hear the front door open and can almost feel the cold air and sense of peril sweep into the house.

Sandra and Veronica freeze and stare at each other, their eyes huge.

Footsteps fill the kitchen.

I envision wet boots and melting snow.

Dad rushes into my room and looks shocked to see Veronica. "What are you still doing here?"

"What's going on?" Veronica says, looking past Dad toward the kitchen.

"Go on," Sebastian says as he pushes Pastor Rick into my room, "may as well see the whole fam-damily."

Pastor Rick looks at me, then at Veronica and Sandra, and shakes his head in quiet regret and disgust.

I feel sick to my stomach.

"You all know each other, isn't that right?" says Sebastian, who has the gun trained on Rick.

Dad is still in his work uniform and coat, and Rick and Sebastian wear heavy parkas. Sebastian wears black dress pants and shiny black shoes that are still covered in snow. It's pitch black outside now.

No one responds to Sebastian, who pulls off his black stocking cap, revealing his mop of matted curly gray-black hair. He stuffs the hat in his pocket and heads for my bed, still holding the gun out toward Rick.

I flinch.

Sebastian laughs. "Happens every time. I tell you, this guy loves me." He squeezes the top of my shoulders with an ice-cold hand, then rubs the top of my head with his rock-like knuckles.

Idiot!

"You've stooped low, Doug, to let your kids get involved in this," Pastor Rick says. "Veronica, I hope you're okay. It's been a long time."

She looks sheepishly at him. "Other than this," she throws her hands up, "everything's peachy." Veronica shoots Dad a look of repulsion.

"Look," Rick says to Sebastian, "you don't need to get Veronica or Hale involved in this—"

"You best shut your mouth, pastor," Sebastian cuts him off.

"Let Veronica leave—"

"I said, shut it!" Sebastian lifts the gun and points it at Rick sideways, like a gang thug. "Sit down in that chair and don't speak another word."

Rick shakes his head and does what Sebastian says.

Veronica starts to walk out of the room.

"Where do you think you're going?" Sebastian says loudly.

Veronica stops and turns to face Sebastian. "I'm leaving." She then continues walking toward the kitchen.

Sebastian blasts a gun shot into the corner of the ceiling.

Sandra screams. Everyone jolts and freezes.

Drywall crumbles to the floor and white dust fills the air.

"Take it easy!" Sandra yells.

"You go sit by the pastor," Sebastian orders Veronica.

Visibly shaken, Veronica scurries for the chair next to Pastor Rick.

"I'll get the money," Dad says. "Just take it and get out of here."

Sebastian shakes his head and sighs. "I wish it were that easy, Douglas." He turns to Sandra. "Get the money from his car in the garage. Bring it up here. Make it quick."

Sandra instantly heads for the door, her cowboy boots clacking across the floor.

When she's long gone, Sebastian looks at Dad and says, "You better keep your eye on that one, Douglas. She's trouble."

Veronica speaks up: "What are you saying?"

Sebastian flashes a smile, arches his back, and rubs a hard hand through his nasty hair. "I like you people. Especially this guy." He nods toward me and pauses, then says, "That Sandra has some . . . demented ideas."

"Like what?" Dad says. "What're you talking about?"

"Just keep your eye on her, that's all I'm saying; especially around your boy."

Veronica and Dad stare at each other with alarm etched in their foreheads.

I would hug Sebastian if I could.

We all hear Sandra coming from a mile away.

Veronica clenches her teeth and seethes.

Dad drops his head and heaves a sigh.

Sandra enters lugging Dad's U.S.P.S. satchel. She walks it to Sebastian, drops it on the floor in front of him, and says, "So what's happening?"

"Open it up for me so I can see it," Sebastian says.

Sandra drops to one knee with a grunt, unzips the bag, and opens it wide.

"So that's fifteen K?" Sebastian says.

Dad nods. "Please just take it and go."

"I've told you it doesn't work that way. These people are ticked. They have a business to run. They make their money on interest. With this fifteen you haven't even paid back the principal . . . Zip it back up."

Sandra does as he says.

Sebastian grabs the strap and drags the bag closer.

"What are we waiting for?" Pastor Rick says.

The room falls silent.

Sebastian picks up the heavy satchel with a grunt and sets it on the shelf behind him, ignoring Rick's question.

"You may as well let me go," Rick says. "You've made it clear I'm not getting the church's money back. Fine. Let me go. I've got a family at home waiting for me."

Sebastian walks to my bed, grips the silver rail with a fat fist and stares at Rick. He digs into his coat pocket and pulls out a phone and examines it. He tosses it to Pastor Rick.

Rick fumbles the phone but holds on to it.

"Text your wife and tell her you're working late. I'll check it—so don't try anything sneaky."

The doorbell rings.

No one moves a muscle.

Eyes search eyes.

Sebastian pats me on the head, takes the phone back from Rick, and heads inside with parting words that send chills down my spine.

"Show time."

22

HALE

The instant Sebastian disappears into the house to answer the door, Pastor Rick dashes for the door leading to my handicap ramp that goes around the side of the house.

"I'm gone," he gasps. "I'll call the police when I can."

He rattles the doorknob anxiously, fumbling to unlock it.

"Rick, he has your car keys!" Dad whispers frantically.

Rick shakes his head as if that doesn't matter.

My heart thunders.

He finally flings the door open. "I'd take you girls, but it would slow me down."

He's gone.

The door shuts hard.

Cold air fills the room.

Sebastian is going to lose it.

Sandra crosses her arms and lowers her head.

Dad examines Veronica, then me. His forehead is etched with fear, his eyes, huge.

There are no voices, only footsteps coming toward us.

"We're out here," Sebastian says softly as he ushers two sinister looking men into my room.

Sebastian notices Pastor Rick is gone, cusses violently, and flies out the door, leaving it blowing in the wind.

The taller of the two men—black hair and mustache, tinted

glasses, wearing a dark suit and long overcoat—walks over to where Sebastian exited and quietly pushes the door closed. He turns and squares up to the rest of us, evaluating the room, squeezing his left fist, then his right, repeatedly. He wears tight-fitting black leather gloves.

The short man—wearing a gray suit, scarf, long wool overcoat—steps into the center of the room wearing shiny black shoes wet from the snow. "Who's Douglas Frodele?"

Dad timidly raises his hand and says quietly, "I am."

The short man takes off his Dick Tracy hat revealing a narrow, bald head. He's clean shaven and seems to have no eyebrows. He also wears tinted glasses with shiny gold frames.

"Who escaped?" says the short man in a low, serious tone as he looks directly at me.

"A friend. A pastor," Dad says. "He's the one who got me the fifteen thousand. It's there—in that bag." Dad points to the satchel on the shelf.

The short man nods at the tall man, who walks slowly over to the satchel, unzips it, examines the contents, nods at shorty, and zips it back up. Shorty chews gum as if in a grinder, making his jaw and cranium shift like a machine.

"Are you the daughter?" Shorty says to Veronica.

Dad starts to answer, "Yes, that's—"

"I'm talking to *her*." Shorty says, still looking at Veronica.

Veronica nods. "I'm the daughter." She nods at me. "That's my brother."

"And you?" Shorty says to Sandra.

She nods at Dad. "His wife."

"Emm. But you're not the mother of these two," Shorty says, pointing at Veronica and me.

Sandra squints at him with a questioning look. "No . . ."

Shorty is obviously in charge. He walks over to my bed and stands over me, staring right into my eyes. "How long's he been like this?"

"About—" Sandra starts to answer, but Shorty cuts her off.

"Dad. I want Dad to tell me."

"Um, it's been a year, about a year," Dad says nervously.

Shorty continues to stare at me.

It seems we are all waiting for Sebastian to return—with or without Pastor Rick.

These two men exude cold-blooded terror. I'm assuming they both have big guns beneath their big coats.

"Uh, if I may," Dad breaks the silence.

Shorty cranes his neck toward Dad as if waiting for more.

"That's half the money in that bag," Dad says. "I will get the other half. I . . . I just need more time."

Lame.

These guys have heard that a thousand times.

They don't even bother responding.

Sebastian made it clear in the past that he was the go-between. Now the real deal has shown up and they mean business. I have to remind myself to breathe.

Shorty orders Tall Guy to collect Dad's, Sandra's, and Veronica's phones. He does so without a word and sets them on the counter by the sink.

They're going to do something. They're going to hurt one of us.

I pray Rick got away.

He'll call the police.

Why did Shorty seem harsh toward Sandra earlier? Could it be that Sebastian told Shorty about Sandra's proposed plan to poison me? Could Shorty have a heart?

Tall Guy heaves a sigh and checks his watch.

Shorty doesn't seem phased.

"He's tube fed, right?" Shorty says.

"Yes," Dad says. "In fact," he looks at Sandra, "has he eaten?"

"I fed him," Veronica says.

Sandra rolls her eyes.

Shorty turns and addresses Sandra. "I was told you know all about tube-feeding."

Bam!

Shorty stares at her.

Sandra's head recoils and she squints at him, her face frozen. She has no words.

Good!

"You want to tell us all what you've been researching . . . about the tube-feeding?"

Sandra's eyes widen and she searches Shorty's face frantically, trying to figure out what he's up to.

He's going to expose her!

Heavy, quick footsteps outside.

The door flings open. Sebastian shoves Pastor Rick into the room so hard he spills to the floor.

Veronica screams.

Then I see why—there's a dark, vertical gash on Rick's forehead two inches long and his face is covered in blood from it.

Sebastian shuts the door and I realize he's holding a gun, which he shoves into his coat pocket.

He must've hit Pastor Rick with it.

Sebastian's shoulders slump and he breathes hard, as if he's just sprinted a 5K. "Sorry about that," he says. "We're all good now."

Tall Guy eyes Sebastian from head to toe and shakes his head slightly in disapproval. Shorty, meanwhile, has turned his back on the mess, crossed his arms, and is looking out the window, squeezing his bottom lip with his left hand.

They are not happy with Sebastian.

Pastor Rick grunts and rolls over into a sitting position in the middle of the floor, leaning over his upright knees. He feels his forehead and brings his hand away glistening with blood.

"Can I get him some paper towels?" Veronica says.

Tall Guy says nothing and apparently doesn't have the clout to do so.

Shorty pivots toward her, gives one concise nod, then peers back out the window, seemingly deep in thought.

Veronica goes to the sink, takes the roll of paper towels off its holder, and hurries it to Pastor Rick. He whispers thanks, tears off a bunch, and presses it to his face with both hands. Once he has most of the blood off his face and a clump of paper towel pressed firmly against the cut, he crawls back to his chair, hoists himself up, and sits with a sigh.

Sebastian crosses to the sink, washes his hands, dries them on a towel that's hanging on the cupboard below, and turns to face everyone.

The tension in the room is palpable.

Each person's eyes dart about apprehensively from one person to the next, except for Shorty, whose back is still turned to all of us.

I'm so petrified that my body suddenly flinches, and I freeze in that position, with my back arched like someone who's just been tased.

Shorty turns to look at me.

My eyes are on his.

He looks deeply at me and grimaces. "We have two problems." Shorty begins talking while still examining me, his arms still crossed. "One is, we only have half the money."

With that, Shorty turns and faces Dad. "We've been patient."

Dad starts to talk but Tall Guy blurts, "Huh uh," and slashes a gloved hand across his throat and shakes his head.

Dad gets the hint and shuts up.

"Your daughter will come with us until you get the rest of the money—"

Veronica cries aloud and covers her mouth as Dad begins to protest—

"Shut up!" Tall Guy steps forward.

Shorty sets his shoulders back, walks across the room, looks up at Sebastian, and says, "Give me your piece."

Sebastian's face morphs into a look of utter surprise. He contemplates saying something but thinks better of it. He reaches into his coat pocket, pulls out the gun, and hands it to Shorty with a worrisome look on his face.

Shorty takes the gun from him by the handle and holds it straight out toward Tall Guy.

Tall Guy walks over and reaches for the gun, but Shorty holds onto it to get Tall Guy's attention.

They look at each other while both gripping the gun.

Shorty gives a slight nod.

Tall Guy nods, takes the gun and, in a flash, grabs Sebastian around the throat and begins forcing him toward the door.

"No!" Sebastian protests and flinches and fights like a coward being led to the electric chair. But Tall Guy, seemingly made of tungsten, manhandles him, forcing him toward the door.

I just want to scream. The tension in the air is too much to bear.

"Don't hurt him," Pastor Rick pleads. "This can all be okay. Please—"

"No. It can't," Shorty says. "This is the second problem."

Tall Guy manages to get the door open and shoves Sebastian outside.

Cold air whistles in.

Shorty looks at Veronica. "You're going to need to pack a bag."

The door closes behind Tall Guy.

"Coincidentally," Sandra says, "she's already packed."

Veronica's mouth drops open and she looks at Sandra in horror.

Dad seethes at Sandra with teeth clenched and eyes on fire.

Phht... phht.

Everyone stops and looks toward the door.

Those were gunshots.

23

DOUGLAS

We're all breathless.

Tall Guy comes back into the house carrying a gun with a silencer. I assume Sebastian is dead in the snow out that door.

My mind reels.

This can't be happening.

You deserve this! You've turned your back on God—it's infected the whole family.

Veronica sees Tall Guy's gun and whimpers, shaking her head in denial and trembling violently. Pastor Rick scoots his chair toward hers and whispers something I can't hear.

Sandra stands there with a somber scowl, arms crossed, shifting her weight back and forth.

I cannot fathom that a man has been shot at my home, in front of my kids.

"Why did you do that?" I plead to Shorty. "Why here? Your problem with him is none of our business."

"You're wrong," Shorty points a finger in my face. "It *is* your business. You strung him along for three weeks. He felt sorry for you, your boy. Then he lets the preacher run . . ." Finally, we see a hint of Shorty's human side, but he quickly recovers. "Why am I explaining this to you?" He raises his chin toward Tall Guy. "Tie them up so they can't follow us."

Tall Guy whips his coat back and holsters his gun. He reaches in his inside coat pocket and pulls out a bunch of thick black zip ties. "The boy too?" he says.

Shorty tilts his head at him and grimaces. "No, not the boy. Does he look like he needs to be tied up? Use your head." He looks around. "Keep Dad in this room; tie him to the bedrail. Put the preacher in the kitchen at the pipes under the sink." He looks at Sandra. "Put cowboy boots in the garage at the water heater."

"What? I'll freeze down there!" Sandra protests.

Shorty narrows his eyes and looks at me. "You picked a real winner, Frodele. I wouldn't trust her with my toothbrush."

Sandra cusses at him, making things even more sickening.

Shorty knows something about Sandra that I don't.

What was that about Sandra researching tube-feeding?

Shorty looks at me. "When will someone show up here next?"

I try to focus on what day it is, on our schedule. "A nurse will be here in the morning." It will be Jasmine. Will they leave the doors unlocked? Surely she'll find us.

Shorty nods at Tall Guy to get going and he jumps into motion, pushing me toward Hale's bed. Meanwhile, Shorty drags a straight back chair over next to the bed for me to sit in. The guy is fire and ice.

He addresses me. "Look, you got half the money, you can get the other half. We see it all the time. People are pressed, they do what it takes."

"Okay, okay, I'll try, but please don't take my daughter."

Shorty heaves a sigh of disgust. "Are you kidding me? You're lucky one of you isn't missing a hand right now. I'm giving you exactly three days. That's final." He looks at Veronica then back to me and lowers his voice to a whisper. "If you don't have the other fifteen grand by then you won't see her again. I'm sorry. That's the way it is."

"Please, can I just—"

"And the bad news is, we won't be done yet. We'll keep coming until we get what's ours. Trust me, you don't want it to get to that."

My head drops in helplessness.

Fear churns in my stomach.

Tall Guy forces my forearm against the bedrail.

"Dad?" Veronica looks at me with an expression of dread and uncertainty that I've never seen in her before.

My heart breaks.

Then a wave of anger washes over me.

Dare I try to fight?

Tall Guy hovers over me, about to cinch the zip tie.

I have nothing to lose.

I ram Tall Guy with an elbow to the gut as hard as I can and lurch toward Veronica.

Out the corner of my eye, I notice Shorty doesn't move a muscle.

Tall Guy snatches me like a ragdoll, cursing under his breath, and shoves me hard toward the chair by the bed. I spill across it awkwardly and it knocks the wind out of me.

Tall Guy whips my arm around and slams my wrist against the bedrail. With a quick, loud *zip*, my wrist is yanked painfully to the bed pole. I'm still gasping for air.

Hale stares at me with his mouth gaping. I see worry in his dark eyes.

"What are you going to do with my daughter?" I cry. "Where will she be? Will you feed her and give her a place to sleep?"

Veronica sobs.

Pastor Rick rests a hand on her shoulder and that makes her cry even harder.

My questions are ignored.

"You're next preacher." Tall Guy motions for Rick to stand up. He does so. "Into the kitchen." Tall Guy walks closely behind Rick into the adjoining room.

Hale flinches uncomfortably and cranes his neck as if watching them walk out.

Veronica and I make brief eye contact and she recoils. I don't blame her. I've gotten us into this mess and she is shaken to the core.

I want to tell her God will protect her, that everything will be okay—but I don't know that, and such words would ring hollow.

Shorty comes over and inspects the zip tie around my wrist.

Then he examines Hale.

If I didn't know better, I would think he has a soft spot for Hale.

Sandra quietly steps over to the door, leans, and glances out the adjacent window toward where Tall Guy shot Sebastian.

Shorty sees me watching Sandra and he looks over at her. "Get away from there! Sit down. Next to the girl."

Like a spoiled child who's been reprimanded, Sandra meanders over and plunks down in the chair next to Veronica with a huff. She pats Veronica on the knee as if wishing her better luck next time at a softball game, and Veronica bucks Sandra's hand away.

Does Sandra not realize the peril we're in?

My God, how did I end up with her?

Cindy crosses my mind. She was so *good.* So wonderful.

The two women are like oil and water.

God is punishing me for my bitterness toward him.

Tall Guy walks back into the room and gets the bag of money.

"It's about time," Shorty says. "Do cowboy boots and we're out of here. Hurry up."

"Come on." Tall Guy waves for Sandra to get up.

Should I signal for Veronica to run?

"You're not tying me up," Sandra says. "I can go with you, make sure Veronica's okay."

"Who do you think you are?" Shorty says. "Tie her to the water heater and let's get out of here. We've been here way too long."

Sandra starts to argue.

"What about the body?" I speak over her.

Shorty sniffs as if he smells rotten garbage. "We're taking him, but it's only because we need you to be getting our money—not sitting in jail."

I picture Veronica riding in their car with a dead body—and what they'll do with that body with her in their presence.

If I tell her to run and they catch her, we'll be in even deeper trouble.

"Please, I'm begging you," I say, "leave her here." Tall Guy has exited with Sandra and the money, so I plead with Shorty. "Take Sandra! Please. Not my daughter."

Shorty ignores me and crosses to the door. He looks out toward Sebastian's corpse, studies the scene, then turns to me. "My advice to you is to get someone over here fast to untie you. Clean that up out there. And get our money. You're so worried about your daughter, just get the money. *Do what it takes.*"

Veronica doesn't have a coat on. She'll freeze out there trying to get away if I tell her to run.

Shorty picks up one of the phones from the counter by the sink and tosses it right back down. *He's going to leave them there.* He figures I'll get to mine eventually. And he knows I won't call the police because of the murder scene outside that door. He only wants enough time to get away and not be followed. Then he wants me free, getting his money.

"Put your coat on, young lady," Shorty says to Veronica.

She looks at me with hopeless, glassy eyes and stays seated.

She's waiting for me to do something!

My heart melts with anguish. "Take me!" I yell. "Take Sandra. Please, not my daughter."

Shorty takes a deep breath and sighs as he looks at Veronica. "Get your coat on, *now.*" He reaches for her arm, but she shirks away, stands, and goes to the coat rack. She slowly puts on her winter coat.

Shorty sizes up the room one last time. "Get your bag," he tells Veronica. Then he looks at me. "You call the cops and she dies. Clear enough?"

Veronica walks over and picks up her overnight bag. She does not look at me.

Shorty escorts her toward the kitchen and turns to face me one last time. "Three days."

24

HALE

They've taken Veronica.

Dad is frantic. His face is covered in sweat and his wrist is bleeding from trying to get free from the zip tie attached to my bedrail.

We both hear a bump outside the back door and freeze.

They are taking Sebastian's body away.

Dad mumbles under his breath and drops from my sight, down to the floor.

I hear the distinct sound of a latch clicking. He's unlocked one of the wheels of my bed.

"Okay, okay," he pants.

I hear nothing more outside the door.

They're gone.

Poor Veronica.

God protect her. Put your angels around her...

Dad is writhing and the bed is jerking. All I can see is his bright red knuckles and fingers and the black zip tie cutting into his bloody wrist. I think he's trying to kick the lock on the other side of the bed, but he'll never reach it.

Pastor Rick yells from the kitchen that we need to get to a phone.

Only believe.

Dad grunts and gets back up, his face dripping with sweat. "Okay, this is going to make a loud noise."

I can't see what he's doing with his free hand above my bed, but I think I know.

Crash!

Yep. He's knocked over the chrome pole that holds my IV pouches.

Now he's back on the floor, probably trying to use the pole with his free hand to reach and unlock another wheel of my bed.

Someone's phone vibrates and alights from the counter over by the sink. I think it's Dad's. Someone's calling him.

He curses and groans. The pole bumps and clangs repeatedly beneath my bed as Dad sighs and huffs and works.

Only believe.

I hear Pastor Rick opening and closing every drawer within reach of him, but if he's indeed tied to the pipes under the sink, he's not near any knives or scissors.

The lock on the other side of my bed unlatches.

"Ahh!" Dad yells. He casts the pole crashing aside, gets to his knees, and finally stands, sweating profusely.

"Okay, Hale, let's hope this works." He grabs the bedrail with both hands and begins to drag my bed around toward the counter where the phones are. The two locks at the bottom of the bed are still latched, but with the top ones free he is actually moving my bed a little at a time.

His phone pulses again from the counter, this time a text message.

"Urgh!" He pulls the weight of the bed with all his might, heaving it about four to six inches at a time. Distress is etched all over his sweaty face.

He drops his head, breathing hard. The hair on top of his head is soaking wet. He keeps his head down, catching his breath.

Slowly, he lifts his head and stares at me. I'm focused on his eyes like lasers.

"Let's do this," he whispers.

He grabs the rails and lets out a loud groan as he sweeps the bed sideways, sideways, sideways. It stops abruptly and he reaches for the handle of a drawer along the counter. He can't get it.

He squeezes the bedrails again and jerks the bed another few inches.

He winces as he stretches as far as he can.

He's got it!

The drawer pulls toward him fast and bangs open. With his free hand, Dad rifles through the contents of the drawer and pulls out scissors!

In a blur, the black zip tie is cut, and Dad is examining the glowing screen on his phone, reading aloud under his breath.

"Are you free? Doug!" Pastor Rick yells from the kitchen.

"Oh my gosh." Dad scrolls frantically and taps his screen. He puts the phone to his ear and his eyes flick to meet mine.

"Gilbert! What's happening?"

Dad waits and listens.

"What? Thank God! Where are you?" Dad yells.

Dad listens intently, his eyes searching the room.

"I'm coming, Gilbert. Stay with them. Don't lose them. I'll be there in ten minutes."

Dad ends his call and puts a hand to his forehead, deep in thought.

What could Gilbert possibly be up to?

Dad crosses to the coat rack, reaches into his coat pocket, and pulls out the revolver he must have bought from Randall. He pops open the cylinder, makes sure it's loaded with bullets, clicks it shut, stuffs it back in the coat pocket, then puts the coat on. Then his hat.

"Doug! What's going on?" Pastor Rick is furious.

Dad inhales deeply, setting his shoulders back, and heaves a sigh, as if he's made a decision.

He steps several feet into the kitchen to address Rick and I'm listening as if my life depends on it.

"Gilbert Spencer was parked outside when those guys took the body and left with Veronica. He knew something was going on here tonight and came to check on us."

Dad's words are quick and sharp.

"Doug, don't just stand there, cut this thing off," Rick says. "I'll help you."

"I can't, Rick. Gilbert's following them and I'm going to get her back."

"Cut me loose, Doug!"

"You'll call the cops, and I can't have that." Dad points to the door in my room. "This is a crime scene and I have to get them their money. You call the cops and everything changes."

"Doug, so help me God, if you don't free me—"

Dad goes into the house.

There's a long pause.

He returns to the kitchen.

"Here's a pillow, water, and crackers. You'll be okay."

Rick screams at the top of his lungs for Dad to free him, but Dad is gone.

The question is, will he free Sandra before he leaves?

25

DOUGLAS

I've never driven so fast in this type of slick winter conditions.

My heart is pounding. All I can think of is Veronica.

Gilbert said he followed her and her handlers down Riverview Road toward the valley and that's where I am.

It's pitch black down here because the streetlights are few and far between. It's heavily wooded and curvy with lots of dips in the roads. The salt trucks haven't been down here lately, so there's probably black ice.

I slow to glance at my phone and call Gilbert while hanging a left on West Bath Road. Gilbert's line rings and his voice comes over my speakers almost immediately.

"They're at the landfill!" Gilbert says. "I'm out front. It would've been too obvious to follow them in. You know where it is?"

"Yeah."

The line is silent.

"Gilbert?"

"I can't believe this, Doug. What on earth—"

"How'd they get in? That place isn't open this time of night."

"They had a key to the padlock and opened the gate. The sign says there's only one way in and out, so I figured it was best to wait here."

"I'm coming. I'm less than two minutes from you. Just keep watching. I'll be right there. If they leave, follow—"

CRESTON MAPES

Gilbert hangs up before I finish. He's mad at me and I don't blame him, but I also don't care right now.

I push the gas harder, flying across a railroad crossing I didn't even see coming.

Slow down or you won't be around to help anyone.

I let up the gas as I glide toward an intersection at Akron Peninsula Road. I can't remember to turn right or left to get to the landfill. I curse and grab my phone. Hands trembling, I open to GPS, examine, and resize the map.

Left.

I toss the phone and gun it.

It dawns on me that Gilbert may call the police.

Just get there!

I'll follow them from the landfill and Gilbert can go home. Maybe I should ask him to check on Hale. I cut Sandra loose so someone could be there for him, but I keep getting a haunting feeling from the subtle comments Shorty made. *What did he say? "I was told you know all about tube-feeding . . . You want to tell us all what you've been researching . . . about the tube-feeding?"*

What was that all about?

I spot the sign for the Akron Landfill in the distance on the right. I gun it one last time, telling myself to stay calm.

As I roll up to the landfill, I see the long horizontal metal gate is wide open, just as Gilbert said.

Headlights flash to my left. It's Gilbert in his Mustang, tucked about thirty yards back from the road. He's pretty much out of sight, except his car made tracks in the snow, which may or may not be spotted by Shorty and company when they exit.

I shuffle through my options and turn left into the snowy grass, following in Gilbert's tire tracks. My car rolls and bumps its way back in toward him. I level off and pull up behind his car, stop, park, turn it off, and get out.

He gets out and meets me between our cars.

"They've been in there for like ten minutes," Gilbert whispers. "I just hope they don't see our cars when they leave."

"Thank you, man, for doing this. You go now. I'll take it from here."

"You need to call the police, Doug! Who are these guys? You can't handle this on your own. What do you think you're going to do? You're not equipped to deal with this."

"I don't know, okay? I just know I need to follow and not let Veronica out of my sight. That's all I know right now. I may call the cops. I don't know yet."

"The police will get Veronica back safely. That's all that matters now!"

"You just go, okay? Thank you for this. I owe you. Now, get out of here before they come out."

"If you want, I'll come with you. We can leave my car here and go in yours," Gilbert offers.

"No. You go."

"Only if you promise me you'll call the police once they get wherever they're going."

Whatever.

"Okay, I will. Now go. Hurry up."

Gilbert sighs and heads for his car. He opens his door and looks back at me. "Do you have that gun with you?"

I stare at him. "Yes."

"If you don't call the cops, I will."

"Don't, Gilbert. Let me handle this. I'll call them. Don't you call them."

He shakes his head. "Be careful." He gets into his car and the engine fires up.

I'm afraid he may call the police right now.

His Mustang rolls through the snowy grass with its lights still off. Once it bumps back up onto the road, it thunders off into the night and its headlights come on a hundred yards down the road.

It's cold and dark and the wind is kicking up.

My footsteps crunch through the snow back to my car and I get in, shut the door, and start it. I roll the windows down so I can hear.

I evaluate my position and pull forward about twelve feet to make sure I'm in the best possible place to hide and follow without being spotted.

It's eerily quiet.

Gilbert's right. What can I possibly do on my own? Maybe I will do as he says and call the police once I find out where they're staying for the night.

I see the beams from their headlights first, lighting up the trees and the snowy landscape.

My heart thunders.

This is it.

26

HALE

I've been on pins and needles ever since Dad took off to find Veronica.
    Waiting.
Listening.
Hoping and praying he left Sandra tied up on his way out.
But that was not to be.
She's in the kitchen.
I don't know if she's freed Pastor Rick or not. They are speaking, but they are talking too quietly for me to understand what they are saying.
I need Rick here. If he leaves—
Oh no...
No.
She's let him go.
Their voices are drawing closer to my room. I can hear them now.
"You guys aren't responsible for that man's death," Rick says. "As far as I'm concerned, all Doug has done wrong is take the church's money, and we'll be as lenient as possible. But those men—they're killers. Veronica is in grave danger."
"You're not telling me anything I don't know," Sandra says, stepping from the kitchen into my room.
Rick follows. His forehead is cut, swollen, and badly bruised

from where Sebastian clobbered him. His face and neck still show smudges of blood.

"Help me with this bed, will you?" Sandra says, rolling my bed back where it belongs. Rick helps her.

"We need to call the police." Rick heads for the sink and tears a bunch of paper towel off the roll, wets it, and wipes his face and neck. Then he turns to face Sandra and dabs at the massive cut on his forehead. "You agree, right?"

Rick goes over to the counter and picks up one of the phones sitting there, then the other, which are Sandra's and Veronica's according to my calculations. He sets them back down.

"Of course," Sandra says. "I'll call them."

She walks over and picks up her phone, turns it on, examines the screen, and scrolls through it.

Rick looks at her. "I guess my phone is still with the guy who died. The software on my laptop might be able to show where it is—that could help us find Veronica."

"I doubt they'd be that stupid—to leave your phone on him," Sandra says.

Rick laughs sarcastically. "This is so messed up. I don't know how you guys got mixed up with these killers."

"It's all about money," Sandra says. "Desperation." She walks over and picks up the IV pole that Dad used to unlock the bed and sets it where it was before.

"I'm going to use Veronica's phone to call my wife and have her bring a spare key for my car. While I do that, will you call the police?"

"Yeah, good idea." Sandra taps her phone several times, puts it to her ear and walks into the kitchen.

They are both talking on the phone at once in hushed tones, but I don't believe Sandra really dialed the police.

She's faking it. I know she is.

Rick is done first. He looks around the room, glances at me, and pats his coat pockets as if making sure he hasn't forgotten anything before he leaves. He steps toward my bed and looks down at me.

Sandra has wandered further into the house, out of earshot.

My eyes are locked on Rick's eyes.

He is just staring at me.

"I'm sorry about all this, Hale." His mouth seals closed and he shakes his head. Tears glisten in his eyes. "What a mess."

My body flinches. I can't take my eyes off his.

Help me, Rick!

He reaches over the bedrail and rests a hand very lightly atop my left shoulder. His eyes are glassy. He closes them. "Father . . . awaken this young man . . . When I knew him before this accident, I know he loved you . . . He needs you now . . . Please, raise him up—"

"Ahem."

It's Sandra, standing in the doorway.

Oh . . . I hate you!

Rick turns to face her. His hand leaves my shoulder.

"Police are on the way," she says. "Is your wife coming?"

"Uh, yeah," Rick says. "She's probably here. We live close."

No.

Don't go!

"You can go through to the front door, out and around," Sandra says.

Rick nods and heads toward the kitchen.

My heart plummets.

Only believe.

Rick stops and turns around toward Sandra. "I will be reporting the stolen money . . . to the police."

Sandra frowns and nods. "Of course you will."

Rick looks at me one last time and lifts a hand. "Goodbye, Hale. I hope to see you again soon."

With that he disappears into the house.

I listen hyper-vigilantly as he walks through the kitchen and around to the front door, exits, and closes the door behind him.

For what seems like a minute of dead silence, Sandra and I stare at each other.

"Does he really think they're stupid enough to leave his phone on Sebastian's dead body?" Sandra says. "That ain't happening."

Slowly, one corner of her mouth turns up into a smile and my body convulses.

"What's wrong wonder boy?" She steps closer to my bed and rests a pudgy hand on the bedrail.

My body is contorted like the St. Louis arch.

"Has everybody gone and left us alone?"

Chills engulf me from head to toes.

She reaches a hand to my hip and tries to flatten me out, but my body is stone cold rigid. She adds another hand, grits her teeth, and says, "Lay down!" while shoving me as hard as she can.

I have no control and can't lay flat.

She puts a hand to my throat. Through clenched teeth she growls, "I am so sick of you."

My left knee bucks uncontrollably and bashes the bedrail, scaring her several feet back from the bed.

She sticks her hands on her hips and shakes her head at me with a nasty, evil glare. "It's about time for your late-night snack, isn't it?" She brushes her hands, crosses to the window, stops, and looks down at the driveway. "Ah, good. There they go." Her head swivels toward me. "Your last hope just rolled out the driveway."

Sandra heads toward the kitchen. "We'll just see what we can drum up for you. Maybe something special. But we can't tell the others, okay?"

No, no, no. Who can show up? Who can stop this?

My heart pounds like a jackhammer as she disappears into the dark kitchen, singing lightheartedly, "When the cat's away, the mice will play . . ."

27

DOUGLAS

When I see the headlights of Shorty's vehicle crest the hill at the landfill, I duck and turn off my car, not wanting them to see my exhaust fumes.

His vehicle glides smoothly down a slope then slows as it approaches the entrance of the landfill.

The large, dark SUV rolls beneath a leaning light pole in the driveway and I make out Shorty behind the wheel. No one is next to him in the passenger seat, so I assume Tall Guy is in back with Veronica.

Sick.

The side windows are tinted so I can't see in.

I can barely breathe.

The SUV creeps through the entry gate and stops just twenty yards from the road. Fortunately, his lights are pointing at an angle about thirty yards in front of my car.

His back door bumps open.

Tall Guy hops out and walks quickly through the snow over to the open end of the long metal gate. With long strides and his breath steaming in the air he swings the gate around, latches it closed, and reaffixes the bolt lock with gloved hands. He double-checks that the lock is secure, then trots back to the SUV, gets in, and slams the door.

They are moving.

I had no chance to see Veronica, but she must certainly be in there or Tall Guy would be riding up front.

Please God, take care of my girl.

My heart is ticking like that of a scared rabbit as the SUV bumps onto the road and roars into the night.

I quickly turn on my car and, with my lights still out, bump through the dark snowy landscape and make my way up to the road. There's not another car in sight. Once I'm rolling on Akron-Peninsula I turn on my low beams and practically jump out of my skin at the sound of my phone ringing.

I glance at the caller I.D.

It is a local number, but one I don't recognize.

I've got Shorty's taillights in sight and I'm staying as far back as possible.

With all that's going on I figure I better answer, just in case.

"Hello."

"Mr. Frodele, this is Randall Bookman."

His rough voice blares over the speakers and I turn it way down with trembling fingers.

"Randall?"

"Yeah, listen, I just wanted to make sure Veronica's okay . . ."

He waits for me to respond, but I can't find any words.

Randall continues. "You said something might be going down at your house tonight. I've been trying to reach her for the past few hours. She usually gets right back to me. I just wanted to make sure everything's okay?"

About three hundred yards in front of me, Shorty comes to the lights of Merriman Valley, a small stretch of high-end retailers and several restaurants and gas stations. It's good to see civilization again. I follow, staying way back.

"No, it's not," I say, thinking maybe there's some way Randall can help me. "The people I owe the money to have taken her—"

Randall cusses and insists I explain.

"They've given me three days to pay the money I owe, or they'll kill her. The thing is . . . I'm following them right now."

"What? Where are you?" Randall yells.

I watch the SUV far ahead.

"Heading up Merriman Road toward Akron."

"Have you called the police?" Randall says.

"Not yet. Right now I'm just trying to keep them in my sight, make sure she's okay. If . . . if I can get the money within three days, everything will be okay."

"Who are these people?" Randall says.

"It started out with one guy named Sebastian. Tonight, two other guys got involved." I can't shake the memory of hearing the silencer fire and picturing Sebastian dead in the snow outside my door. "They're higher up. They mean business. It's not good."

The line goes silent and the only sound is my tires on pavement as we wind our way up into Merriman Hills, with its large estates and sprawling, snow-covered lawns.

Randall sounds like he wants to help Veronica, but he's got that ankle monitor—

"I'm coming over there," Randall breaks the silence, his voice resolute. "Call me at this number in ten minutes and tell me where you are. I'll be close by then."

It crosses my mind about the ankle bracelet, but if he's willing to break the rules, I'm not going to stop him.

"Do you have the Colt with you?" he says.

I tell him I do.

"Good. I'll be armed too."

Wait . . .

"Just stay with them. We'll fix this."

Wait, this is over my head . . .

The line goes dead.

He's coming.

And we're doing this.

28

HALE

Sandra has been in the kitchen and walking around elsewhere downstairs for what seems like thirty minutes.
My nerves are shot.
I'm straining. My temples are pounding. Gilbert's hat has crept down over my right eye. I can't fix it.
I tell myself not to be frantic. To calm down. To only believe.
Be still!
Sandra has been in and out of the refrigerator several times and I heard cupboards opening and closing, glasses clinking, and so on.
My heart sinks into a dark place as I face the fact that the police aren't coming. They would have been here by now. That was all a lie.
She is a witch.
What is she doing?
And what about Veronica?
Where are they taking her?
I want to jump out of my skin!
Dad has created this mess!
Put your angels around Veronica, Jesus. Keep Gilbert safe.
Surely someone has called the police by now—
Wait... Sandra is talking, leaving a message for someone.
Breathe.
Part of me thinks she's simply a mean person who is playing head games with me. That's all, just harmless head games.

But another part of me believes this is real, that she is out to end my life, tonight—the next time she enters this room.

I don't want to die yet. I'm not finished.

I hear myself moaning.

I'm crying.

My hands have crippled up and they are mashed against my chest and throat.

I feel tears on my face.

Where is Gilbert when I need him?

"Golly gracious . . . what is wrong with you?" Sandra enters my room with both hands full—carrying her laptop like a tray, with a drink on it, as well as a pouch of my food. She sets it all down and comes over to my bed.

"Are those tears?" She pulls my hat off, wipes the tears from my face with it, and tosses it aside. She feels my forehead.

"You've worked yourself into a tizzy. My land." She straightens my sheet and blanket. "Lift up." She grunts as she lifts my head up, turns the top pillow over, and smacks it several times to freshen it. "There now."

She goes back over, picks up her things, and sits down in a chair with a sigh. "Your dad's not answering his phone so only God knows what's happening." She sets her drink and the pouch of food down on the small table next to her and opens her laptop.

"It's as good a time to do this as any." Her eyes examine the glowing screen, and she taps and scrolls. "Everyone is going to be better off."

No.

"Your dad and I will be able to focus on our marriage, that's the biggest thing . . ."

No!

She waves a hand in the air. "This room will become a porch-slash-sunroom again."

This can't be happening. She is sick in the head.

"We'll finally be able to get out of debt and save some money. Pay for your sister's college. Save for a wedding—if that day ever comes."

She's going to do it. She's going to poison me.

I flinch.

"Ah . . . you agree, huh?" she snickers.

My eyes burn into her like lasers.

"Best of all, you're going to be in a better place. That's what you believe, right? Mansions of glory and all that? Streets of gold."

She snickers as she tools around on the laptop.

Maybe this is *it. Maybe this* is *my fate.*

"Let's see . . . ah, here it is. It says this young man's death in October 2017 was caused by, and I quote, 'a lethal dose of sodium and vodka injected into his feeding tube.'"

My face is on fire.

My eyes flick to the table next to her and, sure enough, a syringe sits there between the pouch of food and Sandra's glass of clear liquid. I'd missed it before.

My eyes close and my head rolls back on the pillow.

There is only one thing I can do—and that's to cast myself into God's hands and let go . . .

29

DOUGLAS

There are hardly any cars on the road at 9:40 p.m. on a Wednesday night in the dead of winter in Akron, Ohio, so I've dropped back as far as I can from Shorty's SUV, hoping they won't notice me.

Without using his blinker, Shorty turns right on a side street . . . maybe a cut-through to West Market Street?

Since he's now out of sight, I gun it and get to the turn-off as fast as I can so I don't lose him.

It's Cascade Boulevard. I make the right and spot the SUV about a hundred yards in front of me. His brake lights are on.

I pull off to the side of the road and stop.

It's a tree-lined, brick residential street with uneven sidewalks and dated two-story homes situated close to one another. They all have front porches and narrow, driveways that bump up against each other.

He turns left into a driveway.

I'm so nervous I'm slightly dizzy.

I grab my phone. My hands are trembling. I find Randall's number and call him.

"Yeah," he answers on the first ring.

"They just pulled into a house on Cascade Boulevard, between Merriman and West Market."

"What's the house number?"

"I can't see it from here. I'll get closer and text it to you."

"Hurry up, I'm almost there."

"Are you on your motorcycle?"

"Heck no. I'm in my mom's car. Buick Enclave. Red."

I'm hesitant and having doubts about whether I should have gotten Randall involved. "I'm not sure what to do—"

"Just hurry up and get me the address. Are you in the same car you came to my house in?"

"Yes."

"Get me the house number and I'll come in and park right behind you."

The line goes dead.

Okay... gather yourself.

I feel the gun in my coat pocket just to make sure it's there. I put the car in drive and ease back onto the street. It's black and cold outside. Some of the houses are dark, some are low-lit inside, one still has Christmas lights around the front door and mailbox.

I approach the house where Shorty turned in and see his fresh tire tracks in the snow, heading to a separate garage situated about twenty yards off the back of the house; the garage door is down. *He parked in there.*

The house number is eight-seven-three. I drive past the house, down to the end of the street, and pull into the parking lot of a small, triangle-shaped green space; the sign reads 'Brenda Gaffney Memorial Park.' I park and text Randall the house number. Right at that moment, he pulls up next to me, scaring the life out of me. His window goes down. He's wearing a heavy black coat with the collar up and a thick cuffed knit Browns' hat.

"I just texted you," I say.

"I see it," he says. "So Veronica's in that house. You're sure."

My face flushes. "I . . . I'm not positive. They took her from the house and only made one stop on the way here."

"What stop?"

"The landfill in the valley." I sigh, debating how much to tell him. "The two guys that showed up killed a guy at our house tonight —he was their partner. I think they dumped his body at the landfill and came here—with Veronica."

Randall groans and his head drops to his chest.

He doesn't need this trouble.

"The only way she's not in that house is if they got rid of her too, but that wasn't the plan. They gave me three days to get the money. If I don't, then they would . . . you know. We wouldn't see her again."

"So we're talking about two guys in there with her now?" Randall says. "That's it?"

I nod. "Both armed."

"Whose house is it?"

"No idea. Probably an Airbnb."

"Let's go scope it out," Randall says. "Hop in."

I roll my window up, turn the car off, grab my phone, and hurry around to his car. I open the passenger door and the dome light shines down on two large guns—a handgun laying on the middle console, and an assault rifle sitting in the footwell leaning against the passenger seat.

The sight of the weapons gives me pause . . .

"Hurry up!" he hisses.

I get in and shut the door and we are moving.

30

DOUGLAS

We roll up and stop just shy of the house and my phone vibrates.

Randall hears it and looks at me.

Tension sizzles in the air.

I dig it out of my pocket.

Another text from Sandra: "What's going on?"

I stuff it in my coat.

The house is light-colored and has one of those barn-style roofs. There's a small balcony above the front porch; the porch runs the width of the house and features a dark metal awning. A sidewalk goes up the middle of the front yard to a wide set of steps. There's a bench-swing on the porch covered in snow. The front door is wood with three small square windows at the top, and a snow shovel leans next to it.

There are soft lights on downstairs and upstairs, but no hint of movement.

Randall stares past me into the house without a word.

We watch and wait.

He cracks his window, hits a vape pipe, and blows an enormous stream of smoke out the window, much of it coming back in on us with the wind. *Strawberries.*

His hands are dark and weathered, and his cuticles are rimmed with grease.

"You're sure this is it?" he says.

A ripple of doubt runs through me. But I remember where the SUV turned in, I examine the tracks again, and assure him this is it.

"What are you willing to do?" Randall says quietly.

My heart stops. *I don't know!* I stall. "What do you mean?"

"Are you willing to use that Colt, to shoot someone if you have to—to save your daughter?"

I think about Veronica—her safety, her future.

Then I'm hit with a barrage of anxious thoughts about the serious trouble I'm in—the money I owe, Sebastian's murder, stealing from the church, Hale's hopeless condition, my rocky relationship with Sandra, and now, partnering with a felon in Randall Bookman.

I'm overwhelmed.

"Because I'm willing to do what needs to be done." Randall taps the assault rifle. "I got nothing to lose. Veronica's the only thing that's ever meant anything to me."

I had no idea he had such feelings for Veronica. She never indicated it was serious. It's probably one of those relationships where he's always had a crush and she wanted to be friends.

We both look back at the house and, at that very second, a shadow crosses a downstairs room.

We both tense up.

Veronica walks past, followed closely by Shorty.

My heart jumps.

"That's her!" Randall says.

I wait and watch, breathlessly.

Randall unbuckles his seatbelt, grabs the handgun, racks the slide, reaches behind his back with both hands, and tucks the gun in his waistband. He then grabs the assault rifle, hoists the strap over his head so the compact machine gun-looking weapon rests in front of him.

He looks at me. "What do you say? You coming?"

Hesitantly, I reach in my coat pocket, bring out the Colt .38, and stare at it.

Maybe we should call the police.

"You don't have to come." Randall opens his door. "Make a decision! I'm on borrowed time with this ankle monitor."

I look up at the house, searching for Veronica, but no one is in sight.

There's no way I'll get the rest of their money, especially in only three days, which means this is the last chance I have to save my daughter.

Randall bangs his door open all the way. "I'm going."

"I'm coming!" I take a deep breath and open the door.

We both get out at the same time and close our doors quietly.

"Freeze."

The low, calm voice comes from behind us.

Tall Guy.

Phht.

He fires a silencer round into the night sky.

"Stand right where you are, or you're dead."

I instinctively look at Randall, who is standing still, looking straight ahead with his hands out at his sides.

"Hands high," Tall Guy commands. "Frodele, put that gun flat in the palm of your hand and walk *slowly* back here to me. Other guy, you move a muscle and you're on a slab."

I turn around slowly, put the Colt flat in my hand, and walk at a snail's pace toward Tall Guy, hoping a car will come by or that someone in one of these houses will see what's happening.

Tall Guy has both arms out and the gun with the silencer is pointed right at Randall's back.

Snow begins to fall.

With clenched teeth, Tall Guy snatches the Colt from me and jams it in his pocket.

"Go get that AR from your buddy," Tall Guys says. "Slowly lift the strap over your head cool guy."

After a pause, Randall does as he says. He's wearing white sweatpants tucked into big, dark steel-toed boots that are untied; I can't see the ankle monitor so Tall Guy can't either.

I take the heavy gun by the strap and, just as a hope begins to alight in me because Randall still has his other gun tucked in the back of his pants, Tall Guy orders Randall to hand me his other weapons.

"That's all I got," Randall says, still with his back to Tall Guy and holding his hands out to his sides.

"Bring me that," Tall Guy orders me.

I walk the AR to him, still holding it dangling by the strap.

My heart is racing for fear of what Tall Guy will do if he frisks Randall and finds the gun.

Tall Guy takes the AR by the strap and hoists it over his right shoulder so the gun is resting against his back. He says to Randall, "Turn around and face me, cool guy."

With a huff, Randall turns around lazily, keeping his hands out to his sides, and faces Tall Guy. Randall's head tilts sideways and the nonchalant look on his face conveys the message that he is not in the least bit scared. It dawns on me that he must've been in similar fixes a dozen times.

Tall Guy raises his gun toward my head and gently presses the nose of the silencer against my temple. My bowels shrink and my head blares with static.

"If you have another weapon, cool guy, and you don't produce it this *second*, your friend here dies."

Please give him the gun. I'm not going to say it aloud, though, because maybe Randall has some amazing, sinister plan that's going to save our lives—and Veronica's.

I'm so nervous that I taste metal.

"I told you once, I don't have anything else," Randall sneers.

You didn't just say that!

"Check me. Here, look." He opens his coat slowly with both hands.

I just hope Tall Guy doesn't see the ankle monitor. He'll freak.

"Turn around and lift the coat up so I can see behind," Tall Guy orders.

No, no, no...

Randall pauses.

I'm ready to dive out of the way...

Randall slowly begins to turn his back toward Tall Guy, lifting his coat at the same time.

He's going to see it!

At the last second, Randall bolts into action, grabs his gun, and whirls around toward Tall Guy. But Tall Guy, standing still and pointing right at him, has him dead to rights. He fires a silencer round that actually makes a louder noise hitting Randall than it did leaving its chamber.

Randall grunts from the impact, drops his gun, and falls backward into the snow.

Tall Guy cusses and grabs me by the back of my coat collar. He looks around to see if there are any witnesses, then shakes me and marches us over to Randall.

I'm frozen in shock.

There's a splash of dark blood in the snow where he lays. Randall is gripping his left shoulder but says nothing.

"I'd finish you right here," Tall Guys says through clenched teeth, "but I'm not about to carry you. Get up—now!"

Randall works his way to his knees, then to his feet, clutching his shoulder the whole time.

Tall Guy forces me toward the gun Randall dropped. "Pick it up and give it to me."

The gun is cocked. Dare I try to turn and shoot Tall Guy?

I glance at him before I bend down for it and his gun is trained on me.

"Finger and thumb," Tall Guy orders.

I pick up the gun as instructed and hand it to him. He shoves it in his coat pocket and says, "We're walking right up to the front door. Quickly. Quietly. If you try to run, I'll gladly kill you."

31

HALE

Sandra is legit insane.
She just read me two more news stories from her laptop of severe invalids who were poisoned by their caregivers. But she's too *dense* to realize that if she does this to me her fate will be the same as every one of those 'caregivers,' each of whom was caught, brought to trial, and imprisoned.

Sandra sets her laptop down and glances at her phone again, then quickly taps out a text message with her thumbs and sends it. She cusses under her breath and says, "I hope your dad is okay. He's not getting back to me." She looks at me and speaks through clenched teeth. "I swear, if anything happens to him . . ."

She looks away, shaking her head, and talking to herself. She turns back to me and whispers, "In all honesty, between us, I wouldn't mind if your sister didn't come back." She stares at me as if she's waiting for a reaction. "I'm determined to save this marriage. The less interference, the better."

This cannot be real.

She picks up the glass with the clear liquid, holds it up to the light, and swirls it around.

Tell me I'm dreaming this.

"I've actually decided your 'last supper' will be made of a combination of booze and sodium." She sets the glass down, stands up with a grunt, and picks up the syringe.

"I had to watch several videos to learn how to use one of these properly," she says. "It's really quite easy. And, by the way, this isn't going to hurt a bit. You won't even notice it. There will be no pain. You're just going to slip off into la la land. Okay?"

I keep telling myself I'm going to heaven.

He's prepared a place for me.

It will be better.

She picks up the pouch of food and the glass, and crosses to my bedside.

This is it.

Sandra sets everything down along the windowsill.

Why are you allowing this, God? Maybe because if she doesn't do it, I'll spend the rest of my life in this bed. Nobody wants that.

She takes the syringe, pulls the plunger out, pushes it back in to get the air out, and lowers it toward the clear liquid in the glass.

Only believe . . .

She slowly pulls the plunger out. The liquid gathers up into the syringe—

Loud knocking comes from in the house . . . the front door!

My heart stops.

Sandra freezes.

The doorbell rings three times in rapid succession.

Sandra's head swivels toward the sound.

I hear the front door open . . . "Hello?" someone yells.

Sandra curses.

Elation sends chills up and down my whole body.

Footsteps.

"Hello?"

It's Gilbert!

My body bucks.

I groan loudly. It sounds as if I'm in pain, but I'm ecstatic.

Footsteps getting closer.

"What's the latest?" Gilbert breezes in, bundled up, red cheeked, a breath of fresh air from the cold night.

Thank God.

I finally breathe again.

I AM IN HERE

Sandra leans toward me slyly and slides the syringe beneath my pillow, pretending to straighten things.

"Just because the others are gone . . . I can still answer the door," Sandra says. "Sheesh, Gilbert. You scared the daylights out of me, barging in here like that."

"Sorry." Gilbert ignores her and comes over to see me. I can almost feel the cold exuding from him. "Have you guys heard from Doug?"

"No. Why are you here? I thought you were with him."

Gilbert explained that he met Dad at the landfill and Dad didn't want him to stay. It would be too dangerous.

"Have you called the police?" Gilbert says.

"Pastor Rick did," Sandra lies.

With that, my head and shoulders arch back, my crippled arms jab my throat and chest, and I moan.

"What's your problem, Hale?" Sandra forces my head forward and back onto the pillows and, once again, straightens my sheets and blanket as if she cares.

I suppose if Gilbert sees the clear poison in her glass, he'll assume it's one of her regular adult beverages.

I'm guessing it's vodka and salt water.

"Doug told me about the . . . person who got shot," Gilbert says soberly. "Who was it—that Sebastian guy?"

Sandra picks up her 'drink' and the pouch of food, tilts her head and stares at Gilbert. "You know what, Gilbert? It's really none of your business." She walks toward the kitchen. "We did nothing wrong. The police will clear everything up. But right now, you need to get going. Hale's tired."

She disappears into the kitchen.

Gilbert squints at me with a sour, questioning look on his face. He walks around my room where I can't see him.

After a minute he's back in sight. He sees the hat he gave me, which Sandra tossed earlier, picks it up, brings it over, and pulls it onto my head.

Look under the pillow!

Please, please, please . . . God, let him look under the pillow.

Gilbert examines me. He looks over at the windowsill where

Sandra had set everything. Then he looks over at her laptop, sitting closed by the chair. I can tell the wheels in his mind are turning.

God, please, let him figure it out!
Look at the laptop, Gilbert!
Please . . . look under my pillow!

I am staring into his eyes as hard as I can. My neck is straining. I hear myself groan like an idiot.

He reaches over and rests a hand on my shoulder.

"What is it, buddy?"

My shoulders shudder and I cry in frustration!

I hear myself screech deep from within.

"Buddy?" Gilbert pats me. "It's okay. I'm here. Calm down."

Sandra whisks into the room. "What did you do?"

"Nothing!" Gilbert says. "He's agitated about something."

"No kidding. I told you he's tired." She nudges her way between Gilbert and me, rips off my hat, and feels my forehead. "I think he's running a low-grade fever. You need to go, Gilbert. We'll let you know what happens with Veronica. It's all going to work out."

Sandra turns to face him, puts her hands on his shoulders, and turns him toward the kitchen.

No.

"Something's not right," Gilbert mutters, starting to walk, but looking back at me.

Don't go, Gilbert!

"It's been a crazy day. He's over-stimulated. He needs quiet." She keeps shooing Gilbert toward the kitchen. "He needs sleep."

"Put his hat back on, will you? He likes it. Plus, it's cold as heck in here."

Don't go!

"I will, I will." Sandra nods and continues to lead Gilbert toward the kitchen. "And I'm going to text you when I hear anything at all from Douglas."

"I don't care what time it is," Gilbert says.

"You have my word."

Liar!

They walk into the kitchen and their voices fade as she ushers him to the door.

No...
After another moment the front door closes.
The bolt lock latches.
My heart races.
The house falls silent.
Gilbert must've parked out front—she's watching him go.
God, do something!
I groan and stretch and crane my neck toward the window.
It's snowing. Big flakes floating softly down. Lit up by the light from Dad's tool shed.
I get very still. I stare in wonder.
It's so peaceful and quiet out there.
A whisper: *Everything will be okay.*
Footsteps.
Sandra.
"Now . . . where were we, wonder boy?"

32

DOUGLAS

"I'm back," Tall Guy yells as he pushes us through the front door of the house into a large, furnished living room with a fireplace. "We got a problem."

"In here," Shorty yells from another room.

Tall Guy waves his gun toward where Shorty's voice came from, grunts something, and we head in that direction.

The house is warm. It's recently been renovated and is nicely furnished.

Randall and I walk side-by-side. He's clutching his shoulder where he got shot and blood covers his hand and slowly drips onto the light-colored hardwood floor as we walk.

We turn a corner into a small black and white kitchen.

Veronica is sitting on a stool by the sink, surrounded tightly by countertops and no way out. Her eyes are bloodshot from crying, and she weeps even more when she sees Randall and me.

Shorty is seated on a stool at a counter only five feet from Veronica. He's facing her and has her blocked in there. She is not tied up. His gun is laying on the counter in front of him. It too has a silencer on it.

"Stop right there," Tall Guy commands.

Shorty scowls as he examines Randall and the bloody hand covering his bloody wound. Shorty's eyes then shift to the AK

I AM IN HERE

strapped to Tall Guy's shoulder. He looks at me, blinks slowly, and shakes his head.

"This one tried to pull a gun on me," Tall Guy nods at Randall. "I had no choice."

"Who are you?" Shorty says.

Randall stammers and Tall Guy bashes him and tells him to speak up.

"A friend," Randall says, looking at Veronica, then at the bad guys. "Just a friend. Can I take my coat off to look at this wound—"

"What's your name?" Shorty's angry voice cuts him off.

"Randall Bookman."

"How'd you find us, Randall?"

Randall glances at me. He's not saying anything. I'm trying to think of something, but don't want to say anything about Gilbert.

Shorty points at me. "You were zip tied. There's no way you got out of that and followed us from your house." He turns to Randall. "When did you get involved in this? Tell the truth or that shoulder is going to be the least of your worries."

Randall's dark eyes flick to me, then to Veronica.

"Don't look at them!" Shorty yells. "Look at me."

Randall looks at him and I'm thinking, *If I rat out Gilbert right now, they may think they have to silence him.* So, I speak up. "Randall was at our house—in the driveway—when you left. He saw you—"

Shorty lunges toward me and slaps my face hard.

"I want to know from him!"

"It's true," Randall lies. "I came over to see Veronica. We're friends. I saw your car. I saw she was in it. I followed. I called Doug and told him."

"Right," Shorty says sarcastically. "You always drive around armed to the teeth. I don't believe you, you little—"

Randall interrupts him. "Believe what you want, dude, it's the truth."

In a flash, Tall Guys cracks Randall's skull with his gun.

Randall winces, drops to his knees, and covers the back of his head with his free hand. He mutters something under his breath and fights back tears of pain and frustration.

With Randall on his knees, his ankle monitor is exposed!

No... please don't let them see it.

"What the heck!" Shorty cusses, grabs his gun, and crosses to Randall.

"You didn't see this?" Shorty bends over, points his gun at Randall's ankle monitor, and cranes his neck toward Tall Guy. The veins and bones in Shorty's neck protrude grotesquely. "Huh? He's under surveillance! And you shoot him and bring him in here? Moron!"

Tall Guy spits a string of expletives, clenches his teeth, and goes to hit Randall again, but Shorty gets up in his face and shoves him backward. "Stop it!" Shorty says, then shoves him again. "There's no time for that, you idiot!" Shorty flips a wall switch which turns out a lamp in the family room, then dashes to the side of the front window. With his back against the wall, he leans around and peers out the window into the street.

After looking for several seconds, he jerks his head back from the window and drops back against the wall, scowling and glaring at Tall Guy.

"We got cops!"

Tall Guy freaks, points his gun at me, then Randall. "You two get over by the girl. Now!"

Chills engulf me and I get light-headed, thinking he may just kill us all.

I am quick to go over into the enclosed space. I hug Veronica. Randall is bleeding from the head now and slow to get up. Veronica helps him.

"Two of them—in one car," Shorty says. "No lights. Slow drive-by."

"Did they see you?" says Tall Guy.

"How should I know? No, I don't think so."

"These three have seen our faces." Tall Guy paces and tosses his gun from one hand to the other.

Shorty comes back over to us with more agility than I'd given him credit for.

"Check the back," he orders. "See if it's clear."

Tall Guy hurries around the corner, down a narrow hallway, toward the back of the house.

The three of us are standing close together. I have my arm around Veronica, and she is comforting Randall, who is wincing and losing quite a bit of blood from his shoulder and his head.

"He's got to get to a hospital," Veronica whispers, wide-eyed. She's found a white kitchen towel and has him pressing it tight against the wound, but it is soaked with blood. Randall's face is ashen and his lips are dark purple.

I nod at her but I'm thinking we will be lucky to get out of here ourselves.

Tall Guy returns to the kitchen and announces it's clear in back, no cops.

Shorty calls from the front window that the police just parked behind Randall's Buick. "They're running his plates," he yells.

Tall Guy snarls at us and whispers, "You three are dead."

"One of them is getting out," Shorty announces.

The police are here.

We're so close to getting out of this.

"He's got a flashlight," Shorty yells. "He's looking around by the Buick."

"That's blood in the snow!" Tall Guy yells. "They'll call for backup for sure!"

Shorty curses and moves quickly across the family room, gun in hand.

"Get the car," Shorty orders Tall Guy. "Wait, give me those zip ties."

Tall Guy digs the zip ties out of his coat, hands them to Shorty, and says, "We can't leave them alive. You know that."

Part of me is sure one of them is going to turn a gun on us suddenly and—*phht, phht, phht.*

"Shut up! You need to trust me and do what I say! I have to answer to Morgan," Shorty yells in Tall Guy's face, spraying spittle, then lowers his voice to an even, breathy dialogue. "Get the car out of the garage. No lights. Pull as close as you can to the back door. Me and the girl are getting in—"

"They'll see the car—"

"They can't see the driveway from where they're parked. Quit second-guessing me. Now go!"

The tension is palpable, and I feel like I'm floating above the whole scene.

After standing there steaming for several seconds, Tall Guy huffs and stomps toward the hallway. But he stops suddenly and turns back. "They've seen our faces. You need to do what needs to be done." He turns and disappears into the hallway and yells, "If you don't, I will."

I may die protecting Veronica.

Shorty moves quickly, grabs Veronica's bag from a chair, goes to her and pushes it into her gut. "Not a word. We're getting in that car. You're going to do exactly as I say."

He turns to me. "You're lucky I'm in charge." He looks at Randall. "So are you." He turns back to me. "You have two days from tonight to get the money—"

"But you said—" With alarm and fear in my voice, I begin to protest about giving me two days instead of three, but he cuts me off.

"Two days—or you never see her again. And that won't be the end of it. More will die until you pay."

My mind races. My heart drums.

The police are right outside, as close as they'll ever be.

I tilt my head to get Randall's attention. We make eye contact. His hair is wet with blood.

Tall Guy is gone. It's us three against Shorty.

Randall's eyes shift to Shorty, then back to me. I give a slight nod to make sure we're in agreement to try to take Shorty.

But Randall blinks slowly and his head dips.

No!

He frowns and shakes his head. His mouth seals closed, and he glances down at his wounded shoulder, as if to say he's useless. He's pale and looks like he's about to pass out.

I look to Veronica. Her eyes are haunted with worry and her mouth is open in anticipation of what's about to happen. The creases on her forehead give her a look of utter paranoia. Her chin quivers.

I shoot my eyes from her to Shorty and back to her again. I nod at her with a look of revenge on my face, trying to get her on board to fight.

She blinks as if a switch has flipped.

Her mouth closes. Her nostrils flare. She clenches her teeth. Rage has transformed her face and she gives a concise nod.

She understands.

I give Randall one last glance, then Veronica . . . then the two of them make eye contact . . . *we are all on the same page! But I mentally prepare for the fact that Randall may not be much help.*

Shorty scans the family room, then the kitchen. He hands me a zip tie and waves his gun. "Tie Randall to the handle on that lower cupboard right there. Hurry up."

My head spins.

Next, he'll tie me up and take Veronica!

I look down at the zip tie, stalling, stalling . . .

Shorty steps toward me and yells, "Now!"

I look up at him from the zip tie just in time to see Veronica's brown overnight bag loop over her head, pick up speed, and smash Shorty's skull.

He grunts and half collapses but doesn't fall.

I dart for his gun.

He's dazed.

I've got his arm, his thick wrist. The gun is all I care about. It's still in his hand. I back into him with my body, pointing the gun away, into the family room.

I try to back him into the wall, but Shorty is like a building.

Veronica is punching his back repeatedly.

Shorty is strong.

He slashes at Veronica with a free arm. She screams and sprawls to the floor but scrambles right back up.

Randall is on Shorty now.

Shorty is trying to pry my hands away with his free hand. He may do it. He's overpowering.

"Get him!" I yell. "Choke him. Knock him out!"

Shorty is ignoring Veronica's and Randall's barrage of punches and lunges, and is focused on the gun now, too. His strong arms and body are beating at me. He headbutts the back of my head.

I hear pots and pans clanging.

Shorty pauses to stomp Randall's foot as hard as he can, and Randall cries out in pain.

Shorty works an arm around my neck.

Uh oh.

He begins to tighten the vice-like arm around my windpipe and I realize I'm not going to last . . .

With the only strength and consciousness left in my soul, I begin to shake his wrist—hard and fast like a maniac.

This is all I have left.

The gun fires a round into the floor.

I continue banging his wrist.

It fires again.

Glass explodes in the front room.

Everything flips to slow motion.

I glance and see the entire picture window in the front room is obliterated.

The cold black winter night is right there.

"Help!" Veronica screams at a deafening pitch. "Help us!"

Shorty flies back into action, doubling down on getting the gun free, bashing my body, and wrenching my hands away.

If he gets it, we're dead.

I clutch his wrist for dear life, my fingers burning with pain . . . but I'm fading.

"Police! We're coming in!"

Hold on—for Veronica.

The front door busts open.

At that second, *smash!*

Veronica slams Shorty's back with the biggest pan in Ohio.

Somehow, he holds on to the gun.

Sirens.

Another thundering clang rings out like a gong with a grunt from Veronica.

Shorty's body collapses and we both drop to the floor.

His gun skitters away.

I flop onto my back and try to catch my breath.

Randall is also on the floor, laying against the lower cupboards.

"Freeze! Police! Freeze right there!"

I turn and look up at Veronica, who's bent over, hair in her face, out of breath, still clutching the frying pan tightly in both hands with a look of terror on her face.

"Don't move!" a cop yells.

Still on my back, I lift my hands in the air. "Look outside! Outside!" I yell. "One of them's trying to leave! Dark SUV!"

Sirens are louder now, coming from all directions.

33

HALE

Sandra clacks toward me in her cowboy boots, spinning Gilbert's gray ski cap on her right hand while looking at her glowing phone.

"Still nothing from your dad," she murmurs, stops, and looks out my window at the falling snow.

"Look at the size of those flakes. That's good . . . In fact, that's *real* good." She crosses to the door, flips the switch to turn on the exterior flood lights, and opens the door. Almost instantly I feel the draft of cold air.

She examines the area of bright white snow outside the door for a few moments, shuts it, and walks over to me with a chuckle. "Mother Nature is covering up all the mess out there. That's good news. I didn't even have to lift a finger."

She walks around to the other side of my bed, leans over, and roughly puts the hat back on my head.

One last gesture of kindness?

"Lean up for me." She shoves me a bit, reaches all around under my pillow with a few choice words, and finally pulls out the syringe she hid earlier. "There we are. See that?" She wiggles the small instrument right in front of my eyes. "That, my dear, is your ticket to paradise."

My body locks up. I groan like a mummy waking after a hundred years.

"Oh, now you just behave," she says. "The way I figure it, regardless of what happens with your dad and sister tonight, this little chemistry experiment we're about to do is for the best—for everyone. You don't want to be a burden the rest of your life, right?"

My body flinches causing Sandra to jump backward.

"See there? Wow. Something inside you *wants me* to do this." She rests her hand on my head. "You don't want to live like this. This is no life—for any of us."

My heart is failing.

I'm so flustered!

I make an awful screeching sound.

"Okay, you need to relax, Hale." She sounds disgusted. "You're coming apart at the seams." She begins heading toward the kitchen. "When I get back, I expect you to have calmed down. You should be thanking me for this."

She flips a light on as she enters the kitchen.

No one is coming to stop her this time.

She's going to do it.

She's gathering the stuff.

I can't take any more of this.

Part of me wants to just give up. Lay back. Trust. Prepare to meet my Maker, to finally see what's on the other side.

I've thought about it so often.

But another part of me wants to grit my teeth and scream, "This is *my* life! Who are you to take it from me? I am in here! I still have a shot. Miracles happen! My brain is fine! God can heal me."

He must have a plan . . . right?

Don't doubt.

This is no time to doubt.

Only believe.

Sandra's talking in the kitchen. It must be someone on the phone. I can't quite make out the words.

God, please, you need to do something. Stop her!

She's coming.

I trust you. This is on you!

"We have got to scoot." She comes in quickly with her arms full, carrying the pouch of food, syringe, her phone, and the infamous glass of clear liquid. "Your dad called. They're safe. They're okay. He got Veronica. The police are involved, but that's okay."

Thank God. Okay, that's good, that's good.

"The police are bringing your sister home soon." Once again, she lines everything along the window sill. "Your dad is going back to the station to answer some questions. Now, I need to text our friend Gilbert and let him know everything is okay, so he stays out of our hair."

As I watch her rapidly punch in a text message using both thumbs, the phone glowing close to her face, I feel something stirring in me.

My neck seems to release. My head rolls to the side. The snowflakes are falling peacefully, like white feathers.

"That takes care of that." She tosses the phone onto the shelf, hooks up the g-tube to the port in my stomach, and quickly flushes the system with water.

My face burns and my forehead breaks out in a sweat.

Only believe.

"That hooligan Randall Bookman got involved. Got himself shot. Idiot." Sandra mumbles to herself as she retrieves the syringe, withdraws the plunger, pushes it all the way back in to get the air and remaining liquid out, then dips it into the clear drink. "I think I can pull this off to look like a seizure; they happen all the time to people in your condition." She leans closer and whispers, "But I don't care if your dad figures out that I did this, I really don't."

Ever so slowly, she pulls back the plunger, drawing the liquid up into the syringe.

"He'll realize in a few weeks—well, maybe it'll take a month or two—but he'll realize this set him free. I'm not worried about the finances. He won't be either, anymore." She finishes loading the syringe, leans over the bedrail, and looks into my eyes. "Because *you* won't be around any longer to leach us out of every last red cent we bring in."

I blink several times and swallow.

If she does this, it was meant to be, and I'll be in a better place.

Sandra whispers to herself as she carefully pierces the top of the pouch of food with the needle of the syringe.

I feel a strange sense of unmistakable clarity.

Suddenly, I inhale deeply . . . so deeply and violently that my chest expands as it never has. My back is arched and my shoulders set back and dig into the bed, erect as a soldier.

Sandra's head cranes back and she glares at me with furrowed brow.

She's frozen like that, as if she's seen an apparition.

I exhale long and loud, sounding creepily primitive.

"What is *that* all about?" Her voice cracks when she says it.

Her face contorts with creases of fear and doubt.

I clear my throat, which surprises me, because I'm never able to do that.

A slight squeal escapes from Sandra's lips.

As if these things are happening one by one to shock Sandra—like on one of those hidden camera shows—my rigid arms suddenly go limp; they drop peacefully to my sides.

She lets out a whimper.

Next, my crippled hands relax. My fingers gently unfold.

Sandra's eyes have enlarged and are fixed on the metamorphosis taking place before her.

"What the heck is going on?" She practically cries as she says it. Her lips and chin quiver.

She blinks repeatedly and shakes her head as if trying to snap out of it.

"This ends now," she says in a breathy whisper, virtually panting.

With trembling hands, she focuses back on the syringe and food pouch. All she has to do now is inject the poison, hang the pouch, and turn on the pump.

Her eyes meet mine.

Her forehead glistens with sweat.

Her breathing is choppy.

My head turns away, toward the syringe in her hands.

"That's right," she hisses. "Time to go."

As her thumb begins to depress the plunger to release the venom into the bag—my right hand jolts and seizes her wrist.

She screams.

The food bag drops to the bed.

My head turns back to her face—now contorted into a mask of horror.

She looks as if she's been struck with five million volts of electricity.

My hand is clenched to her wrist like a vice—and is tightening.

The rest of me cannot move, cannot do anything.

She cries out for help, for me to stop, but I cannot stop.

The syringe drops next.

She pounds the bed with her free hand and tears streak from the corners of her eyes.

"I'm sorry, I'm sorry," her voice quivers. "Please, stop. Please. You're hurting me!"

I am a machine.

As my grip cinches tighter, the expression of panic etched on her face becomes more and more alarming.

She begins to try to pull away, to pull free.

She strikes me several times, but hitting my body is like hitting beams of wood.

She is so alarmed that she begins trying to yank her wrist free and actually jerks the bed several inches with each yank.

But every ounce of hatred she has dumped on me in the past year has funneled into the muscles in my crippled hand, which now clamps her wrist like an industrial bench vice. So focused am I on that pressure point that stars swirl in my vision.

She is crying now.

And . . . she is tiring.

She slumps over the rail of my bed, bawling now, and still locked to me like a trailer hitch.

She gets a second wind and leans as far away from the bed as she can, pulling hard at my hand, and stretching a leg out to drag the closest chair toward her. She cries out trying to snag it with her foot.

I've still got her good.

The chair tips over.

She blurts out a string of expletives, then drops to her knees. All I can see is her grotesquely bent, purple hand that is still bolted to

I AM IN HERE

mine where a bright red ring now appears. Her hand jerks as she sobs and sobs.

I am laying flat, looking straight up at the stippled ceiling.

I am not tired.

I feel like I can hold her like this forever if I have to.

I look down. All of the evidence against her lays right here next to me—the poison-filled syringe, the pouch of food with the hole in it. And along the windowsill, the glass of what I think is vodka and sodium.

Wait... I think...

Yes.

Sirens.

Thank God.

Sandra flinches.

The police are closing in.

I'm going to make it.

With a grunt, Sandra gets back to her feet.

She hovers over me, her face dark with gloom and wet from crying.

With her free hand, she picks up the syringe, glances at me, leans over to the windowsill, and shoots its contents back into the glass. She looks at me again. Her nostrils flare. Her mouth, which is sealed shut, shoots a quick trembling grin, which disappears in a flash.

She wiggles the syringe at me, then kneels, disappearing out of my sight, pulling hard at my hand, which still has her wrist tight.

I hear a snap.

The sirens draw closer.

She gets to her feet again, holds up the syringe, and raises her eyebrows at me. The needle is broken off. She slips the harmless syringe into the front pocket of her jeans.

I see blue lights painting the trees in the night outside my window.

Sandra picks up the glass and lifts it toward me as if to say "cheers," and downs the clear liquid.

Her head drops. She winces and coughs violently, partially spraying me with the foul-smelling concoction.

She smacks the glass down on the windowsill and wipes her

mouth with the back of her free hand.

I count two cop cars. They are now in the driveway.

Coming in.

She takes the food pouch with her free hand, stretches over, and hangs it on the IV pole.

No one will think anything of it.

In their eyes, she has done no wrong.

I am the violent one here, the invalid maniac.

Loud knocking.

"Police!" they yell from outside the front door.

My defeated eyes meet Sandra's.

"You gonna let me get that?" she smirks.

I squeeze her wrist harder and harder until she squirms, then release her, and look away, into the snowy night.

34

DOUGLAS

It's very late and I'm several miles from home. It's snowing hard, the salt trucks are out with their orange lights flashing, and the roads are thick with fresh fallen snow. I'm taking it slow, gathering my thoughts as I drive; relieved to be free, for the time being.

I told the police everything. In doing so, a proverbial weight has been lifted from my shoulders. I told them I borrowed twenty-thousand dollars from Sebastian, owed him thirty thousand, and couldn't pay it back. I told them I talked Pastor Rick into giving me fifteen thousand out of the church benevolence fund. They said he had contacted them about the matter, and he was not sure yet whether the church was going to press charges against me.

I told the police Shorty and Tall Guy showed up at our house tonight, threatened us, killed Sebastian, and kidnapped Veronica. The two thugs are being held in the county jail without bond until their indictment.

Are there people higher up than them in the 'organization' who are going to want to collect the money I owe? I'm afraid there probably will be. I don't know what I'm going to do about that. I could be in jail myself for committing fraud against Pastor Rick's church.

When I told the police about Sebastian's murder, they immediately dispatched officers and investigators to our house. They will be there by the time I arrive home. They also sent a team to the landfill where I'm assuming Sebastian's corpse ended up.

Randall Bookman was taken by ambulance to Akron General Hospital and is going to recover. I explained to the police that he helped save Veronica's life, and mine, and it looks like he won't be in any further trouble with the law for venturing outside the boundaries of his ankle monitor.

Veronica, after answering questions at the station, was free to go and instead of heading home, requested to be taken to the hospital to see Randall. I don't know where she is right now. She could still be with him, or she could be at the house.

A massive snowplow approaches and I pull off to the right shoulder of the road as he scrapes past loudly, adding to the four-foot wall of snow on the side of the road.

I hope Sandra fed Hale.

Perhaps now she and I can start over.

That's never going to happen.

I'm in such deep thought I almost miss the turn onto our road, but I pump the brakes, slow, and ease onto our street.

Sandra said she wanted our relationship to work, that she wanted it to be like when we first met . . .

But Hale was well when we started dating.

Everything's changed.

And, deep down, I know she's not good for me. She's negative. It's almost as if she scorns Hale. And she and Veronica fight like cats and dogs.

It's time to end it.

That prospect fills me with shame.

But then I could focus on making things right with Veronica and Hale, maybe even start going to church again; somewhere new, where no one knows us.

From several hundred yards shy of the house, I see blue police lights flashing in the night sky, reflecting off the tall trees, and my heart begins to beat faster.

Pulling into the driveway and heading up the incline, my car hits an ice patch and lists. I immediately stop, pause, put it in reverse, and ease back down to the street. I put it in low gear and try again, aiming for snow instead of ice this time. I get traction and the car slowly climbs. Finally up on level ground I see three police cars and two other unmarked cars parked at all angles.

The flood lights are on up at the side door leading to Hale's room, and the area is corded off with yellow police tape. There's also a bright light on a tripod. A man and woman in long coats wearing gloves and hats, likely investigators, are tiptoeing around up there with flashlights and iPads.

The driveway to the garage is blocked by their cars so I pull off to the side of the shed as far as a I can, ease to a stop, park, turn the lights out, and the car off.

I drop back and sigh.

Silence.

Cold silence.

Considering the alternatives, things are about as good as they could be, for now.

I lean forward with my hands on top of the steering wheel. I rest my head there, taking a deep breath, and exhaling.

It's so quiet.

So still.

My mind feels clear—for the first time in a long time.

After sitting here a minute, I decide it's time to come clean.

"I've been running from you," I whisper. "Dissing you. Trying to live as if you're not here. Wanting to forget you."

The words from the long-forgotten Psalm arise from someplace deep in my soul: *Where can I go from your Spirit? Where can I flee from your presence? If I go up to the heavens, you are there; if I make my bed in the depths, you are there.*

"I've turned my back on you. I've *hated* you. Because of Cindy and Nate—and Hale . . ." Tears flood my eyes. "But there's nowhere else to go. You're it. You're the only way. Forgive me for my bitterness. Please. Wash it away. Bring me back to you. Bring me back home."

I use the remote to open the garage door from my car and trudge through the snow. Quietly, I make my way through the garage and up the dark stairs into the kitchen. No one has heard me. I stand here evaluating the situation.

The place is lit up like a stadium. Sandra is seated in a chair in Hale's room talking to a male police officer opposite her. He is black, very fit, with an erect posture. He takes notes on a small clipboard as they speak in hushed tones. Sandra is holding one of her wrists. Her face and eyes are red, and her hair is a mess. She's been crying.

Why?

My attention turns to Hale.

The air in my chest leaves me.

He is lying on his back and his whole body is straight. His head rests on the pillows and he is looking up at the ceiling. His arms and hands are resting at his sides.

I realize my hand is covering my mouth and tears have filled my eyes.

I step into the room.

Sandra notices, glances at me, and resumes her conversation with the officer, holding her wrist up to him, which has a grotesque purple ring around it.

"What happened to Hale?" I say as I approach his bed.

The officer looks up to acknowledge me, but Sandra keeps on talking to him.

Beyond the door leading outside, the two investigators are squatting over an indented patch of snow, and a photographer is taking photograph after photograph with a big camera.

The officer across from Sandra holds up a hand to try to pause her dialogue, then stands, steps toward me, and introduces himself as officer Philip Dunn. He asks who I am.

I tell him who I am as I continue toward Hale's bed.

Sandra gets up and follows me.

"What happened?" I ask for the third time.

"He grabbed me!" Sandra blurts. "When I was feeding him." She points to a bag of Hale's food, hanging from the IV pole, and to the portable pump laying on his bed and the g-tube still attached to the port in his stomach. "He wouldn't let go of me! For anything. He was like a madman. He wasn't conscious. He was . . . like a robot. If he could have, he would have killed me. Look at this."

She holds her wrist up to my face and turns it back and forth. "Your son did this!" It is indeed a gruesome bruise that seems to be changing colors and spreading as we speak.

Laying there looking almost peaceful, Hale's eyes move from the ceiling to my face. His whole body is still.

He stares deep into my eyes.

"Look at him," Sandra says. "He's not himself."

Officer Dunn has turned to converse with one of the investigators.

I lean over the bed and touch his face with the back of my hand. "What's up, bud? What's going on?"

"Why'd you try to amputate Sandra's hand—that's the real question," Sandra hisses. "I need a good stiff drink."

"Not now you're not," I say as I disconnect the g-tube from Hale's port and hand it to Sandra along with the small pump. Then I notice the glass on the shelf by the window. "It looks like you've already had one," I say.

Sandra huffs and turns away, interrupting Officer Dunn to ask how long they'll be here.

Hale is still glaring at me.

The second he knows he has my attention again, his eyes move from mine, across the ceiling, over to the opposite side of the bed, toward the IV pole.

I go around the bed and reach for the pouch of food hanging there.

It's warm.

Ugh . . . My hand is wet.

I look down.

The pouch is leaking onto my hands.

That's weird.

I instinctively look up from my wet hands to Sandra, who is staring at me.

Her head snaps away the second she sees me looking at her.

"Why is this leaking?" I say as I cross to the counter to throw it away and dry my hands.

"How should I know?" Sandra meets me over there, sets the tube and pump in the sink, grabs a towel, and pushes it toward me.

I throw the bag of food in the trash, take the towel from her, and wipe my hands. It's sticky so I use soap and water to wash my hands in the sink.

Something's not right.
Why was that bag leaking?

Officer Dunn approaches me. "Mr. Frodele, I'm going to need to talk to you for a few minutes. Can we sit down over here?"

"Yes." I finish drying my hands and Sandra shows up at the sink with the glass that had been sitting over by Hale's bed.

The doorbell rings twice, then pounding, then the front door opens.

"Doug?" a male voice calls. "Doug, you've got to see this!"

Gilbert flies into Hale's room waving his phone in the air.

He's wearing no coat, just jeans, a sweatshirt, boots, and a black ski cap.

His eyes are huge and he's out of breath.

"You've got to see this!" Gilbert scans the room, glares at Sandra, then looks back to me. "The police need to see this!"

35

HALE

Normally, all of the people and commotion in and around my room—the lights, the talk, the motion, the static from police radios—would have driven me into a spastic frenzy.

But an incomprehensible peace has come over me.

It's inexplainable.

I'm not the same as I was before I grabbed Sandra's wrist.

Progress has been made, a big chunk of progress. It's as if I've taken a giant leap forward, toward being myself again. I'm not there yet. My body can't do what I want it to. But I've changed somehow.

My head rests softly against the pillows. My arms and hands are straight and relaxed at my sides, which never happens.

Gilbert has just blown in, waving his phone, breathing threats against Sandra, and summoning Dad and the nearest police officer.

"Make sure she doesn't try to run," Gilbert says on edge, jabbing a finger at Sandra. "I have evidence against her, right here on my phone. She tried to poison Hale."

Sandra cranes her neck backward, squints a sour look, and laughs. Then she plunks down in a nearby chair with a sigh.

Officer Dunn introduces himself to Gilbert, insists the boy slow down, and writes down Gilbert's name, age, and address.

"After all that happened here earlier tonight, I came back to check on Hale," Gilbert says. "Then I went home and fell asleep. But when I heard the sirens, I knew to check my phone."

"Slow down, son," says Dunn. "I'm going to need you to back up."

Sandra smirks and drops her head as if Gilbert is telling a fable.

Officer Dunn's police radio chirps and a voice beckons him. He excuses himself and turns his back. "This is Dunn. Go ahead, Randy."

"We found fresh tire tracks in the snow at the landfill. We have a body." Static. Pause. Static. "Two gunshot wounds, as witnesses heard. One to the chest, one to the head."

Officer Dunn ends the radio contact and turns back to Dad and Gilbert, who are standing near my bed, and near Sandra, who is seated. "Continue, please," Dunn says.

Gilbert glances at Sandra, then squares up his phone to Officer Dunn and Dad. "I'm just going to start playing this. It speaks for itself."

Sandra shifts uncomfortably.

Gilbert holds the phone in front of the two men and hits play. It must be a video because Dad and Officer Dunn lean in for a closer look at the screen.

"Lean up for me," comes Sandra's voice. "There we are. See that? That, my dear, is your ticket to paradise."

That was when she held the syringe up to my face.

Sandra suddenly stands and shoves her chair back loudly.

Officer Dunn and Dad are gaping at Gilbert's phone.

"Oh, now you just behave," Sandra's voice continues. "The way I figure it, regardless of what happens with your dad and sister tonight, this little chemistry experiment we're about to do is for the best—for everyone. You don't want to be a burden the rest of your life, right?"

My heart thunders. I'm relieved, but I'm also concerned about what Sandra might do right this instant.

Over the video I hear my bed lurch from my reaction to Sandra's evil threats.

"See there? Wow," she continues. "Something inside you *wants me* to do this. You don't want to live like this. This is no life—for any of us."

Sandra cusses, examines Gilbert's phone, looks up and scans the bookshelf on the far wall. "You little . . . you can't do that! That's invasion of privacy. It's against the law!"

"Sir," Gilbert raises his voice to Officer Dunn, "please watch her. She *will* try to run."

Officer Dunn pulls a chair next to him and tells Sandra to sit down, which she does hesitantly while cursing under her breath.

Gilbert crosses to the bookshelf that Sandra was looking at, pats around, and snatches a small black camera that fits into the palm of his hand. "I left this earlier, because of all the chaos going on—and because she was acting so weird."

Yes!

Gilbert comes back over. "I'm going to fast-forward here because this is when she goes into the kitchen to prepare the poison."

"You don't have any evidence!" Sandra squawks. "Where is this dastardly 'poison?'"

As Gilbert works his phone, Dad runs a hand through his hair and glares at Sandra with fury in his eyes.

"Oh, now you're big and tough," Sandra says to Dad. "That's unlawful. It's eavesdropping. It won't be admissible."

"Here we go," Gilbert holds the phone back up to the two men. "She just came back into Hale's room after hearing you and Veronica were okay. She texts me that everything is fine, and then, here, watch."

He hits play.

"I think I can pull this off to look like a seizure; they happen all the time to people in your condition." It's Sandra's voice on the video. "But I don't care if your dad figures out that I did this, I really don't."

As Gilbert continues playing the video on his phone, Officer Dunn and Dad watch aghast as Sandra explains that Dad will eventually be glad that she killed me. After that, she pierces the food bag with the syringe, and I grab her wrist. Gilbert fast-forwards to where she empties the contents of the syringe into the glass while I'm still holding her, breaks the needle on the floor and stuffs the syringe in her pocket, then drinks the glass of clear liquid.

Gilbert stops the video. "I'm almost out of battery."

Officer Dunn instructs Sandra to stand and empty her pockets.

"No way, I want a lawyer!" she yells while remaining seated.

Dad bolts for her. He grabs her and wrestles her to her feet, knocking her chair over. Officer Dunn steps in quickly and digs a hand in one of the front pockets of her jeans.

"You are so dead for doing that!" she screams and rips her arms out of Dad's grasp.

But Officer Dunn holds up the broken syringe and says, "What's this?"

Dad steps toward him, examines the instrument, buries his head in his hand, and turns away in disgust.

Gilbert seizes Sandra's laptop and marches it to Officer Dunn. "There's more evidence on here," Gilbert announces. "Earlier in the video I shot, she reads to Hale about invalids who've been poisoned by their caregivers—and how they did it."

Dad suddenly turns toward my bed. He races over, right next to me, turns on the light on his phone, and drops to the floor on his hands and knees.

"This is all so illegal," Sandra says, pointing to her laptop. "That's private property. You can't take that."

"Pipe down, ma'am," Officer Dunn says. "Turn around. I'm placing you under arrest—"

"Arrest! For what?" Sandra steps toward him. "Get outside and do your job. A man was murdered here tonight and you're chasing rabbit trails."

Dad gets to his feet and holds a hand in the air. "I found the needle."

Sandra lunges for Officer Dunn's gun.

Her hands are on it and I think she's about to fly loose with it and start firing.

With a fast right hand, Officer Dunn jams the gun into his holster as hard as he can, pressing down on it so she can't remove it.

They grunt and wrestle and stagger. Like a bolt of lightning, Officer Dunn punches Sandra's throat with his left fist, which resembles a sledgehammer. A ghastly noise like a windpipe cracking escapes from Sandra and she drops to the floor like a sack of flour.

I close my eyes.

It's over.

I hear Dad hugging and praising Gilbert.

I hear the metal of handcuffs clinking, then latching, and Officer Dunn speaking, out of breath. "Sandra Frodele, you are under arrest for the attempted murder of Hale Frodele. You have the right to remain silent..."

EPILOGUE

HALE

It's May and winter is finally over. It looks glorious outside. The snow has melted. I can almost smell the rich green grass from here in my bed by the window. The sky is cobalt blue, and the spring breeze gently blows the new foliage coming in on the trees.

I'm still praying for a miracle—that one day I will be able to walk through that thick grass in my bare feet and feel that refreshing breeze on my face. Land a good job. Get married...

Ever since the incident that winter night when Sebastian was killed here at the house and I grabbed Sandra's wrist, I have remained in the same state. My body is relaxed. I am calm. But I cannot communicate. It feels like I should be able to move as I wish, to talk, to hop right out of this bed and run.

But I can't.

Not yet.

Dad and Veronica are rushing about in the kitchen. I hear glassware clinking, brief conversation, quick footsteps, and the smell of toast. They are getting ready to leave for Veronica's graduation. She receives her associate degree this afternoon from The University of Akron, and she has a new job lined up with a land surveying company based in Copley. Several of her girlfriends are trying to convince her to get an apartment with them in Fairlawn Heights, but she confided in me that she wants to be near me —and Dad.

I AM IN HERE

Here comes Jasmine, whistling into my room carrying a laundry basket piled so high with clean clothes she can barely see over the top.

Veronica and Dad follow her in. Dad has a mouthful and is carrying a plate with a sandwich and pretzels on it. Veronica is eating a huge piece of toast slathered in peanut butter with slices of banana on it, which she carries precariously on a napkin.

Jasmine comes over and, with a grunt, opens the window next to me and goes back to folding clothes.

The cool breeze feels glorious.

"You're going to be sitting around a long time if you come with me now," Veronica says to Dad. She wears a beige dress, gold earrings, and brown heels.

"What the heck, I'm off work," Dad says. "I may as well go with you."

"You better go!" Jasmine says. "Get out of here while the getting's good."

Jasmine is an angel. She's always been good about shooing the family out of the house while she's here so they can have a break from all the tedious caregiving.

After the incident with Sebastian, Dad somehow managed to get his old job back as head of client services at the shipping company where he'd worked for sixteen years. He's back making the big bucks.

When Shorty's and Tall Guy's replacements eventually showed up one evening in late March, Dad was ready for them. Thanks to his new job, he'd secured a home equity line of credit and was able to stroke them a check for thirty thousand dollars. From what I gathered—after quite a bit of back-and-forth—they allowed him to write the check to a small handyman company, which they'd created as a cover through which they could receive the funds. Anyway, it seems that monkey is now off our backs for good.

"Do what you want." Veronica holds out her black cap and gown on a hanger and eyes them up and down. Her eyes are bright and she's smiling. "I know there's a Starbucks near the venue. You can hang out there till the doors open."

"There you go," Jasmine chimes in.

Dad and Veronica have been getting along remarkably well lately. With Sandra out of the picture, we've become more like a family again. They've even started going to church together, which blows my mind. They tried a few, then one Sunday Veronica said she was going back to visit Crossroads. Against his better judgment, Dad went with her. Pastor Rick gave the sermon that Sunday and they've been going there ever since.

Even before that, Crossroads did not press charges against Dad, so he's feeling like a new man. I think the merciful way Pastor Rick treated Dad, and the grace the church showed him, enabled him to go back. In fact, that unconditional love may be what ultimately drew him back to the church, and to God.

"What time will you guys be back?" Jasmine says.

Dad looks at Veronica and raises his eyebrows. "What do you think, home by five or six?"

"You'll probably be home by then, but Gilbert's taking me out to celebrate," Veronica says with a wink and a chuckle.

Jasmine and Dad tease her about that and it makes me laugh inside along with them.

"He's coming today, you know, to the graduation," Veronica says. "I told him he could sit with you."

Gilbert still goes to Crossroads, so Veronica has been seeing a lot of him there, too. If I'm honest, I'm a tad jealous. After all, he is my best friend and I don't want his relationship with Veronica to interfere with our weekly meetings.

On the other hand, my heart soars when I think about the possibility of Veronica and Gilbert ending up together. She couldn't ask for a better man, and we couldn't hope for a better addition to the family.

The doorbell rings.

"I'll get it." Jasmine scurries into the house, a bundle of energy.

"I got a text from Sandra," Veronica says, out of the blue.

"When?" Dad says.

"This morning." She sets the remains of her sandwich down on her napkin, licks her fingers, and hands Dad her phone. "Big sob story."

Dad examines the glowing screen of Veronica's phone, reading the text. After a moment, he hands the phone back to her.

"I can't believe she remembered you're graduating today," he says.

"She's got her reasons," Veronica says. "She's probably trying to get back on good terms with you because you got your job back."

After Sandra was arrested in this very room back in February, bond was set and someone in her family bailed her out. She's free and awaiting trial for the attempted murder of yours truly. Of course, the court slapped a restraining order on her so she can't come near any of us.

"She's not supposed to contact us, is she?" Veronica says.

Dad shrugs. "No. But that seems harmless enough. Just don't respond."

"Oh, really?" Veronica whines sarcastically. "Darn. I wanted to text her back and tell her how much we miss her. Gag me. Loser."

"Look what we have here!" Jasmine comes floating in with a small, but beautiful bouquet of flowers. "For the graduate!"

"What?" Veronica takes them with a happy look of surprise on her face. Her eyes are dazzling.

Gilbert has really fallen for her.

"Oh brother," Dad says.

"We have an admirer!" Jasmine squeals.

Veronica sets the flowers down and opens the little white envelope. Holding the small card with both hands, she silently reads the message.

A hand shoots to her mouth.

Tears flood her eyes.

When she looks up at Dad, tears streak down her face.

She hands him the card.

Dad takes it and reads it. He frowns and shakes his head.

"Well? Don't keep us in suspense," Jasmine says.

"Can I read it to them?" Dad says.

Veronica nods.

Dad looks back at the card and reads it aloud: "'Veronica, congratulations on your graduation. I know great things are ahead for you. Have a wonderful life.' And it's signed, 'Randall Bookman.'"

"Well, I'll be," Jasmine says. "He's the one in prison, right?"

Veronica and Dad nod but say nothing.

After a four-week trial, Randall was one of five young men

convicted of armed robbery. The verdict came down just about a week ago and he is now in the Mansfield State Penitentiary awaiting sentencing.

"He really loved you, didn't he?" Dad says softly.

Veronica chuckles and cries at the same time. "What's not to love?"

Laughter rings out and fills the house.

Jasmine is laughing.

Dad is laughing.

Veronica is laughing . . .

Suddenly, all of their eyes light up and their faces turn to me in shock.

Because I . . . I am laughing, too.

WHAT'S NEXT FROM CRESTON?

If you're ready to start Creston's latest series, check out book one in the Signs of Life Series on **Amazon**:

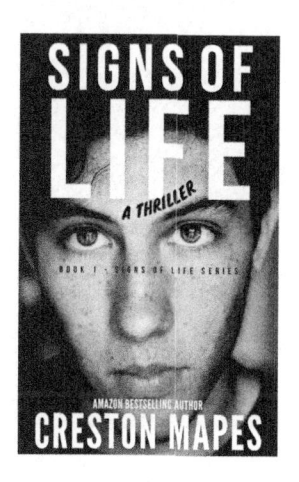

* * *

If you'd prefer to start another series by Creston, The Crittendon Files is a must-read. Book one is Creston's all-time bestseller, *Fear Has a Name*.

WHAT'S NEXT FROM CRESTON?

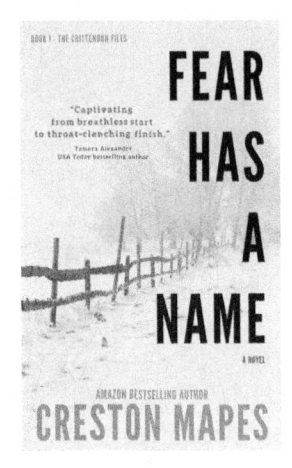

* * *

Another fan favorite mystery-thriller and bestseller of interest:

* * *

ABOUT THE AUTHOR

Creston Mapes grew up in northeast Ohio, where he has fond memories of living with his family of five in the upstairs portion of his dad's early American furniture store - The Weathervane Shop. Creston was not a good student, but the one natural talent he possessed was writing.

He set type by hand and cranked out his own neighborhood newspaper as a kid, then went on to graduate with a degree in journalism from Bowling Green State University. Creston was a newspaper reporter and photographer in Ohio and Florida, then moved to Atlanta, Georgia, for a job as a creative copywriter.

Creston served for a stint as a creative director, but quickly learned he was not cut out for management. He went out on his own as a freelance writer in 1991 and, over the next 30 years, did work for Chick-fil-A, Coca-Cola, The Weather Channel, Oracle, ABC-TV, TNT Sports, colleges and universities, ad agencies, and more. He's ghost-written more than ten non-fiction books.

Along the way, Creston has written 13 contemporary thrillers, achieved Amazon Bestseller status multiple times, and had one of his novels (*Nobody*) optioned as a major motion picture.

Creston married his fourth-grade sweetheart, Patty, and they have four amazing adult children. Creston loves his part-time job as an usher at local venues where he gets to see all the latest-greatest concerts and sporting events. He enjoys reading, fishing, thrifting, bocci, painting, pickleball, time with his family, and dates with his wife.

To keep informed of special deals, giveaways, new releases, and exclusive updates from Creston, sign up for his newsletter at: **CrestonMapes.com/contact**

To view all of Creston's eBooks, audiobooks, and paperbacks go to **Amazon.com/author/crestonmapes**

STAND ALONE THRILLERS
I Am In Here
Nobody

SIGNS OF LIFE SERIES
Signs of Life
Let My Daughter Go
I Pick You
Charm Artist
Son & Shield
Secrets in Shadows

THE CRITTENDON FILES
Fear Has a Name
Poison Town
Sky Zone

ROCK STAR CHRONICLES
Dark Star: Confessions of a Rock Idol
Full Tilt

Printed in Great Britain
by Amazon